W9-DIV-560

Isabelle's
Boyfriend

Isabelle's Boyfriend

Caroline Hickey

ROARING BROOK PRESS

New York

Text copyright © 2008 by Caroline Hickey
Published by Roaring Brook Press
Roaring Brook Press is a division of Holtzbrinck Publishing
Holdings Limited Partnership
175 Fifth Avenue, New York, New York 10010
www.roaringbrookpress.com

Distributed in Canada by H. B. Fenn and Company Ltd.

Library of Congress Cataloging-in-Publication Data
Hickey, Caroline.
Isabelle's boyfriend / Caroline Hickey. -- 1st ed.
p. cm.
Summary: When fifteen-year-old Taryn meets the perfect guy and finds
out he is dating someone else, she befriends his girlfriend and dates his
friend, only to realize the hurt she has caused to her old friends.
ISBN-13: 978-1-59643-413-4
ISBN-10: 1-59643-413-9
[1. Best friends--Fiction. 2. Friendship--Fiction. 3. Dating (Social cus-
toms)--Fiction. 4. Conduct of life--Fiction.] I. Title.
PZ7.H5258Is 2008
[Fic]--dc22
2008011134

Roaring Brook Press books are available
for special promotions and premiums.
For details contact: Director of Special Markets,
Holtzbrinck Publishers.

Book design by Jaime Putorti
First Edition September 2008
Printed in the United States of America
2 4 6 8 10 9 7 5 3

Chapter One

When I get home from school, the dog is scratching at the back door, demanding to go out and pee. She may look like a sweet, furry marshmallow, but really she's a bully. A ten-pound, purebred, bichon frisé bully.

"Camille," I say, "it's snowing outside and I'm in my uniform. Can I please change first?"

Camille cocks her head and gives me a meaningful stare, one that says, *You know it's your job to walk me right after school. I've been home alone all day. My bladder hurts.*

"But it's *cold* outside," I tell her. "Can't you go in the toilet like a normal person?"

No, because I'm not a person. I'm a dog. And I will pee on the living room rug and make you clean it up if you don't walk me right now! She gives the back door another scratch for emphasis.

I glance outside at the flurries, debating whether to change out of my loafers and school jumper. By now Camille is yowling as well as scratching, so I just zip up my jacket and grab her leash. "*Fine,* mutt. Let's go."

As we navigate down the slippery driveway, my mom pulls up in her car and lowers the window. "Hello, chickies!" she calls. "How goes it?"

"Great," I reply halfheartedly.

"Did Mommy's little girl have a good day?"

I don't answer because this is directed at the dog. Camille puts on her biggest smile and hops around on her back feet to let Mom know she's happy to see her, too.

"Take her all the way to the stop sign, Taryn," Mom says. "They'll salt the roads soon and she won't be able to walk around."

I swear my mom thinks I'm an idiot. Like I don't know Camille will lick the salt off her paws and get sick.

"And you really should put her parka on," Mom continues. "It's too cold out for her."

"Mom, she's fine. We'll back in a few minutes, okay?"

She shakes her head at me and waves at Camille before raising the window and coasting up the driveway.

Small, hard flakes are coming down and a thin layer is dusting the road and trees. The sky is somewhere between pale pink and gray. Everything is quiet and still and peaceful, like Camille and I are the only two people on earth. I don't want to give her the satisfaction of knowing I'm enjoying being outside, so I tell her to hurry up and pee.

She obliges and we both pause to admire the yellow stain

on the snow. For some reason, even though it's dog pee, it seems special because it's on the first snow of the year.

It's so beautiful out I decide we might as well walk past the stop sign and go a little farther down the road. My school loafers have no traction and I slip and slide as we walk, snow seeping through my soles. No cars have driven down this way yet, so I can't see where the road ends and the grass begins.

I'm leaning my head back to catch a snowflake on my tongue, when out of the corner of my eye I see someone walking toward us. It's a he, and as he gets closer, snowflakes swirl around him, sticking to his hair and jacket.

When the guy is right in front of us, he stops. We're the only ones out in this beautiful, snowy white world and I hold my breath, feeling like something very special is happening but I don't know what it is.

The guy has dark hair and dark eyes and he stands there in the snow staring at Camille and me. He's really good looking, but not in a model or actor way. More like a guy that might be the lifeguard at your pool.

"Hey," he says. "That's some dog."

I glance at Camille, who is groomed to look like an oversized white powder puff. "Yeah," I say. My voice comes out thin, like watery spaghetti sauce.

"You should be careful—you might lose her in the snow." He smiles.

This guy is *smiling* at me. I don't know what to do, so I laugh loudly, even though his joke wasn't that funny.

"So," he says. He's still smiling. It's amazing. His smile radiates some kind of megawatt energy. I can almost feel it hitting me in the face. "I'm Epp."

"Epp?"

"John Epplin. But everybody calls me Epp."

Epp. Possibly the coolest nickname I've ever heard. "I'm—I'm Taryn," I stammer. "Greenleaf. But nobody calls me Green."

It's not the funniest thing anyone's ever said, but it's not bad, considering. Epp laughs and I feel taller. Cooler. Prettier.

"You live around here, Green?" he asks.

I try to come up with a witty reply but I don't think there is one for such a simple question. So I say, "Yeah, down the street."

"And who's your little friend?"

I look at my dog. I've certainly never thought of her as my friend. "This is Camille. My mom calls her my sister, but I haven't found any evidence of a blood relationship."

"She's . . . fluffy," he says. "What kind of dog is she?"

I can't believe we're discussing Camille. I'm standing two feet from this unbelievable guy and we're talking about *Camille.* "She's a bichon frisé. They were originally bred as pets for royalty, but this one was bred just to irritate me."

Epp laughs again but this time he also gives me a look. A look like he's *looking* at me, like he's actually considering me. Me, in my knit hat with the pink pompom on top, and my blue polyester uniform and sweater tights.

I have to keep talking to him. "Do you live around here?"

"No—my girlfriend does. She's skiing with her family this week and I'm taking care of their dog."

He says the g-word casually, like it's nothing. Meanwhile, my insides freeze like I swallowed a snowball. I finally meet a guy and he's talking to me and looking at me and it's snowing, and he has a *girlfriend*. "Your girlfriend?"

"Yeah, Isabelle Graham. You know her?"

I nod, a smile stuck to my face. Sure, I know Isabelle. We've gone to Eastley Prep together since kindergarten. She's the kind of girl who floats around on a big, pink, fluffy cloud of perfect. She's never had a frizzy hair day or a D in Biology or even a sore throat, probably. She's one of the most popular girls at school, and we're only sophomores.

"I'm walking her dachshund after school all week," Epp says. "I'm on my way there now."

"Oh." I stuff my hands in my pockets and pray silently. *Please, please let him ask me to join him. Please, please, pretty please.*

"Do you . . . " His voice trails off as Camille abruptly pulls away from me, tugging hard at her leash, and nearly yanking my arm out of its socket.

I'm five feet four, and Camille barely clears fifteen inches, but her willpower could move a school bus. I plant my feet but my loafers won't stay put on the slick layer of snow. A second later, I'm flat on my butt, icy slush soaking through my jumper.

"No, thanks, Camille," I say, trying to sound casual while sprawled across the road, "I don't want to make snow angels right now."

Camille ignores me and continues tugging for home. I try to stand up but every time I put a loafer down, it shoots out in front of me. Finally, Epp offers me his hand and pulls me to my feet. For five seconds, we're glove to glove. I look into his eyes, which aren't just ordinary dark brown. They have a lighter hazel ring around the outside, like some kind of fancy dark chocolate with caramel icing.

"Th-thanks," I say, in my watery-spaghetti-sauce voice. Camille jerks my arm backward as I talk. "I guess Camille wants to go home."

"Too bad. Well, Green, I'm sure I'll see you around." He gives me one last smile, then turns and strolls toward Isabelle's house, kicking up snow as he walks.

"See you," I call weakly.

Camille gives the leash another tug and I let her pull me down the street. My butt is soaked and freezing, but I barely feel it.

"We're back," I yell when we get in the house. I carry Camille to the kitchen sink to rinse her paws. She fights with me while I pick off the tiny snowballs clinging to her fur.

"Taryn, make sure you wash her feet," Mom calls from the den. "They'll be salt—"

"I'm doing it, Mom." Honestly, you'd think the dog was the Queen of England.

I towel dry Camille, dump her on the floor, and run up to my room. My feet and butt are numb from the snow, so I peel off my wet uniform and throw on jeans, a sweatshirt, and some woolly socks.

Then I hit speed dial one on my phone.

"Helllllooo?" Lila likes to stretch out her hellos. She thinks it makes her sound sophisticated. It doesn't.

"You're never going to guess what happened," I say.

She thinks a minute. "Umm, you got an A in Trig?"

"No—better."

"You talked your mom into letting you go to a coed school?"

"C'mon." She knows my mom adores Eastley. And single-sex education. "You're not even trying to guess."

"You've decided to join the circus?"

"*Nooo*," I say impatiently. "I met a guy. A really cool, funny, hot guy."

"Taryn liiikes a boooy," she sings. "That's great! When are you going out?"

"Going out? I just *met* him." Lila somehow believes that relationships happen as easily as they do on television, even though neither of us has ever had one. "Anyway, don't get too excited—he has a girlfriend."

Lila groans. "Ugh. That's lame."

"Yeah. And guess who the girlfriend is? No, don't guess, your guesses are annoying. I'll just tell you—Isabelle Graham."

I hear a gasp. "Eww! No!"

"Eww, *yes*. Isabelle Graham with her perfect skin and perfect B-cups."

"She's not that perfect," Lila lies, cracking her gum and chewing. "I want to hear about *him*. What's his name?"

"His name's Epp, John Epplin, and he's got dark hair and eyes and this intense smile. I met him walking Camille. He's walking Isabelle's dog after school all week. The Grahams are skiing."

"I know," says Lila. "She was talking about it in American Studies last week. They're up at Blue Knob."

"Ooooh," I sneer. "*Blue* Knob." Only really annoying people take a week off to go skiing in late November when school is in session. People like Isabelle Graham.

"Gross," Lila agrees. "Tell me more about *Epp*. What'd you guys talk about?"

I try to recall our conversation, but mostly I just remember his smile. "Our names, and Camille. And Isabelle—barf. I think he liked me, though. He called me 'Green' and he kept smiling at me, this *huge* smile. And he helped me up when I slipped . . . "

Lila oohs and ahhs. "Sounds romantic. What were you wearing?"

"My uniform," I say. "Camille had to pee and she wouldn't let me change first."

"Are you serious? You've got to stop letting that dog boss you around. She's affecting your personal life."

"TARYN!" my mom yells from downstairs. "Come set the table!"

"Speaking of bossing me around, my mom's yelling at me," I say. "Gotta go. See you tomorrow."

I float downstairs, still thinking about Epp, and set the table. Since it's just Mom and me, it takes about five seconds. I don't know why she has to make such a big deal about me doing it before dinner's ready. Especially since we're having leftover lasagna for the third day in a row.

"We're supposed to get a few more inches tonight," Mom says, placing a dinner plate with fresh boiled hamburger and peas on the floor for Camille. The plate is fancy blue china and it's not part of a set we own. She bought it just for the dog. "Snow this early means we'll have a cold winter."

I fork some lasagna and splatter sauce on my sweatshirt. "I hope they don't close school tomorrow."

"Pardon me?" Mom asks. "Are you *my* daughter?"

"Lila and I are starting Driver's Ed tomorrow night," I remind her. "And I don't want it to be canceled." I pat my sweatshirt with a napkin but the sauce stays put.

"Just make sure it doesn't interfere with your home-work—you have exams coming up."

I give up on the stain and go back to eating. "Not until after Christmas break. And I'm only worried about Latin and Trig."

"Latin will help you on your SATs next year."

"That's just a myth adults invented to make us study a dead language. A dead, hard, impossible language."

Mom frowns so deeply her eyebrows touch. "Maybe you shouldn't have gone to see your father over Thanksgiving. You should have stayed here and started studying."

The mention of my visit to my dad's hangs in the air for a second, and I concentrate on chewing and swallowing. "It's not like I chose to go, Mom. I visit every other holiday. You guys came up with the arrangement, not me."

"Don't be snappy, Taryn," Mom says mildly.

"I'm not snappy. I'm just *saying.*"

"Well, say more nicely."

"Sorry," I say, but I'm not. I don't particularly like having to take a train all the way to northern New Jersey to see my dad. I wish he'd stayed in Baltimore with us. But he didn't, and I hate that my mother makes me feel bad every time I go see him.

Camille licks her plate clean and starts jumping on my mom's legs, begging for more food. It's amazing she only weighs ten pounds.

"Push her off you, Mom. We've got to teach her not to beg."

"Now, now. Don't pick on our baby. Camille missed Mommy today, that's all." Mom pulls Camille up into her lap and plants a big kiss on her snout. Camille ogles Mom's plate of lasagna.

I roll my eyes and start clearing the table. My mother's a smart woman, with seemingly normal brain chemistry, but Camille has a way of turning her into mush and making me feel like a third wheel in my own house.

Chapter Two

Lila's mom drops us off at We Brake for New Drivers driving school. Lila insisted we go here because supposedly this is where all the guys from the boys' schools go. I guess being tucked away at Eastley for ten years is starting to get to her, because she's become obsessed with us meeting guys.

"This is it, Taryn," she tells me as we walk in. "We're here. With them."

The school is in a strip mall and looks like it hasn't been redecorated for several decades. The chairs are those cruddy one-arm school desks and the walls are covered with wood paneling. The whole place smells like tires. It definitely doesn't live up to the glamorous experience Lila's been fantasizing about.

She pushes me toward two seats near the back of the classroom. "So we can see everybody," she explains.

We sit down and Lila surveys the room. "Taryn," she whispers, "check out all the school jackets. That way you'll know who's worth talking to. The guys from Filbert Hall are jocky and dumb, the St. Ivan's guys are jocky and *cute*, and the guys from Landers Prep are smart but need a few more years to mature."

"What? Says who?"

"Says Mary." Mary is Lila's older sister, who also went to Eastley and is now away at college. "Watch out for the girls in the maroon jackets—they go to Sinclair, St. Ivan's sister school, and they think all St. Ivan's guys belong to them."

I realize then that Lila is proudly wearing her Eastley jacket. I wonder what it says about us. School jackets are a big thing in Baltimore, since so many kids go to private schools, but I've never paid much attention since the only people I ever hang out with also go to Eastley.

A clipboard with a sign-in sheet gets passed around, and I carefully print *Taryn Greenleaf* on it. I pass it to Lila, who glances at the names of the guys sitting around us, and then flips to the previous page to see a list of names from a different class.

"Taryn!" she shrieks. "He was *here!*" She points at the sign-in sheet, and I lean over to read it. One of the names is John Epplin of, where else, St. Ivan's. "Maybe we'll run into him one night."

"*Shhh*, Lila, calm down. Did you notice the name beneath his?"

She glances back at the sheet to where it says *Miss Isabelle Graham.* "Eww," Lila says. "She wrote 'Miss'? Who does that?"

"I don't know, but they were together. If they go on Driver's Ed dates, then they are *really* together."

"We're at Driver's Ed together. And we're not *together*."

I glare at her. "Even if they weren't *together*, I still wouldn't have a chance with him."

"I disagree—you have a chance with anybody. But let's focus on the positive, okay? There's a whole room of available, soon-to-be-driving guys here."

I scope out the room and see a few possibilities, but none of them have Epp's smile. Or his chocolate and caramel eyes. More importantly, none of them are looking back at me.

An overweight man steps to the front of the room. "Hello. Tonight our topic is, 'Driving in Inclement Weather.' Anyone here know what 'inclement' means?" His voice is flat and sounds like he's reciting a script.

"It means," he continues, without waiting for an answer, "severe, harsh. Like snow. Or rain. Or wind. Or hail. We're going to watch a movie about this. Then we're going to take a short quiz. If you sleep during the movie, you won't pass the quiz. No talking."

He flicks off the lights and a movie appears on the projector screen. I try to concentrate, but it's distracting to sit in a room full of guys. They make a lot of coughing and sniffing noises, and they scratch their faces and pass notes to each other. And they all have really big feet.

However, if Eastley Prep has prepped me for anything, it's multiple-choice tests. I watch about five seconds of the movie and still manage to pass the quiz.

Mom and Camille pick us up at nine o'clock. Mom never goes anywhere without Camille. She brings her to the grocery store, the florist, carpool—everywhere except work.

"Hi, girls," she says as we climb into the car. "Did you learn a lot?"

"Oh, definitely," says Lila. "There were a lot of really smart people in the class. I learned just by watching them."

"Good for you, Lila," Mom cheers. "That's the spirit."

I shake my head. Lila's such a suck-up.

"Hey Miss Squirmy, calm yourself," Mom says to Camille. She's trying to drive while holding her, and Camille's angling for a good view out the window. "Taryn, what did you learn?" she asks.

"That you shouldn't drive with a dog in your lap."

"*Taryn.* You know Camille loves to go for car rides. Would you rather I left her at home all alone?"

I nod yes in the backseat at Lila who stifles a laugh and looks out the window. "I guess not," I say unconvincingly.

"Now, tell me something you talked about in class."

"We learned what 'inclement' means. I'm sure it'll come in handy on the SATs."

--- ~ -

During a free period the next day, Lila asks me about my follow-up move with Epp. Apparently his Driver's Ed date with Isabelle didn't faze her.

"Move? There's no *move*. There's no anything." I open

my American Studies book and pull out some paper, hoping she'll drop the subject so I can start my essay.

"Why not? You should try to run into him again today— you know he'll be in your neighborhood."

"No, thanks. I'm not a stalker."

"Who said anything about stalking?" Lila sounds offended. "I'm saying go walk Camille at the same time and place as you did on Tuesday. Isabelle will be back this weekend, so this might be your only chance to run into him again."

"And why would I want to do that?"

Lila looks at me incredulously. "Because you guys clicked. Because you're meant to be together."

"He has a *girlfriend*, Lila."

She folds her arms across her chest and shakes her head at me like I'm a naughty three-year-old. "Taryn, this is so like you."

"Like me how?"

"To give up and just accept the circumstances. This is the first guy you've ever really liked, and you're not going to *do* anything."

This is classic Lila. She thinks she can trick me into doing whatever she wants me to do by telling me I'm a wimp. It usually works. "The *circumstances* are that he has a girl-friend. And who cares anyway? What do I want a boyfriend for? I have a very busy and exciting life."

She looks at me sideways and we both laugh loudly. A few girls sitting nearby shoot us dirty looks. Even though it's a free period, everyone is studying and not talking, be-cause that's what you do at Eastley.

"Just walk Camille by Isabelle's house today," Lila whispers. "That's all I'm saying."

I shake my head and try to work on my essay, but I can't focus. Lila does have a small point. What's the harm? So I walk Camille past the stop sign again, maybe wearing something cute. If I see him, I say hello, and if I don't see him, Camille gets a nice walk.

It's not as if guys like Epp come along every day. I've managed to go fifteen years without meeting one. I've had some awkward slow dances at mixers, and some conversations with the friends of friends' boyfriends, but I've never met a guy I couldn't stop thinking about. A guy who made me feel better and smarter and cooler just by standing next to him.

———

By the time carpool drops me off at home, I've decided to do it.

I unlock the back door, toss my book bag on the floor, and completely ignore Camille. She has her paw in door-scratching position, but I run right past her and up to my room to change.

I unzip my inflammable polyester jumper and tug on my most fitted jeans—the pair I can wear only if I'm going out for a little while, and definitely not if I'm going to a movie, because there's no way I can sit in them for two hours. Then I layer a cotton T-shirt under a pink fuzzy sweater, knot a pink-striped scarf around my neck, and brush my hair out. I add some blush and eyebrow gel, so I look fresh but not makeup-y. I throw on my fitted brown leather jacket that's not very warm but looks good, and run back downstairs.

Camille is scratching impatiently at the back door. I clip on her leash and she gives my outfit a withering look, as if she can smell my desperation.

"What do you care what I'm wearing?" I ask her.

I don't care, Camille sniffs at me. *You're just so obvious.*

"Look, you're getting a nice long walk, so lose the attitude." Camille makes a low, growling noise and I open the back door. We walk briskly down the driveway and head in the direction of Isabelle's house.

As we slowly approach the magical spot where Epp and I met, I feel my stomach tense up. Most of the snow has melted, revealing bare, anorexic trees and lots of potholes. The road is lined with puddles of brown slush. It's a lot less romantic than I remember and I wonder if I exaggerated the meeting in my mind. It seemed so special, so momentous when it happened. But now, looking at the empty street and the cold white sky, I just feel stupid.

"Camille, am I crazy? What am I doing here? He probably doesn't even remember meeting me."

Camille looks thoughtful for a moment, like she's considering my words. Then she pulls me to the side of the road to sniff a bush. She squats to give it a quick spray and then starts walking in the direction of Isabelle's house. Since we don't normally walk that way, it's clearly a sign.

"You're right, Camille. We're here, so we might as well walk by." I follow her four furry white legs, knowing I'm officially crossing into the tiniest bit of stalker territory. Lila would be proud, but that's not exactly a comfort.

When I see Isabelle's house, I hang back. The lights are on and there's a car in the driveway. Did the Grahams come back early? Or are they the type who put their lamps on timer when they're away? I look at Camille to see if she's willing to give me another sign, but she's watching a squirrel.

As I'm debating walking by or turning around for home, Isabelle's front door opens and a dachshund trots out, followed by Epp.

He's here. I'm going to talk to him again.

My heart starts thudding and I frantically try to think of something to say. Then, as quickly as it started, my heart stops. He's not alone. Isabelle is behind him, pulling the door closed. She and Epp start walking in my direction, their arms around each other's waists. Their hips bump awkwardly but they don't let go.

Camille sees the dachshund and yips excitedly, dragging me toward them. There's no way I can turn around now and disappear, or even casually stroll by. We get closer and closer. Isabelle glows. Her face is sun kissed; her long red hair is silky and straight. Her lips are the perfect shade of Chapstick pink.

They're standing three feet in front of me.

"Hey, Taryn," Isabelle says. Her tone is friendly and natural, like this isn't the first conversation we've had all school year.

"Hi." I glance at Epp, not sure whether or not to say

hello to him. He looks just as good as I remember. Maybe better.

"This is Epp, my booooooyfrrrriennnd." She draws out the word *boyfriend* for about six seconds.

"We met the other day," Epp says. "I met Camille, too."

Camille looks up at Epp and smiles bewitchingly, the way she does at my mom. I feel a flip-flapping in my stomach like I swallowed a live fish. He remembered Camille's name! That's got to mean something.

"You did?" Isabelle's eyes dart to Epp, then back to me.

There's an awkward pause. "I thought you were skiing this week," I say to her.

"We were. We went to meet my brother—he had a long Thanksgiving break from college—but he bailed on us early, so my parents decided to come home."

"That's too bad." I try to sound sincere, but I don't really care that her perfect-family skiing trip got cut short. I'm just waiting to see if Epp will say anything to me.

Her dachshund moseys over to Camille and starts sniffing her butt. Camille, uncharacteristically, allows her to and even seems to enjoy it. The three of us watch uncomfortably.

"Mitzy, that's not nice," Isabelle scolds. "Leave the doggy alone."

"I think they like each other," Epp says. "Maybe we should give them some privacy."

Isabelle looks uncertainly from me to Epp. "But they're both girl dogs! Girl dogs don't do that."

"Sure they do," I say. "It's very trendy right now, especially with smaller dogs." I smile and feel a balloon in my chest when Epp smiles back at me.

Isabelle frowns at the dogs and Epp elbows her. "She's kidding," he says. His eyes meet mine again. Like we have our own private joke and Isabelle isn't in on it.

"I *know.*" Isabelle pulls on Mitzy's leash and pivots Epp with her arm. "We've got to take Mitzy for her walk," she says. "See you at school."

Epp's eyes hold mine for one more second. Then he waves good-bye to Camille and Isabelle drags him down the street, their hips bumping together again.

Chapter Three

In the cafeteria before first period the next morning, I tell Lila about running into Epp and Isabelle. I think maybe I exaggerate the eye contact too much, because Lila gets pretty excited.

"He *what*?" she yells across the cafeteria.

"Shhhhh!" I hiss. There are only a few students in here, but still. She needs to get a grip. "We don't need to announce it to the world."

"He *gazed* at you, Taryn," she says, clutching my arm. "He remembered your *dog's name*."

"You're starting to sound like one of those psycho women they have on talk shows." I'm mostly kidding, but I'm sort of serious, too. I can practically smell how badly she wants us to get boyfriends. "I'm sorry I even told you. Let's just forget it."

Lila smears cream cheese on a bagel and shakes her head at me. "You're so pessimistic, Taryn. I'm amazed you get out of bed every morning."

"I'm not a pessimist," I snap. "I'm a *realist.* The guy is taken. I might as well start flirting with one of those dumb Filbert Hall guys at Driver's Ed, because this guy is off-limits."

Lila sighs. "They did seem pretty stupid, didn't they? And they all had that weird, too-long hair. "

"Yeah, like they think they're going to be cuter just because they can grow hair. Guys are depressing." I tear off a piece of her bagel and pop it into my mouth.

"Driver's Ed's not what I thought it would be, but don't worry, I'm cooking up a new plan already," Lila assures me.

"What new plan?"

"We're going to a St. Ivan's football game tomorrow," Lila announces. "And I'm not taking no for an answer. It's the perfect opportunity to mingle. *And* to run into your new friend."

"He's not *my* friend," I remind her. "Anyway, I thought only the girlfriends of St. Ivan's guys went to their games. Other girls that go just look desperate."

Lila waves her hand. "Whatever. You don't think a stadium full of guys would be happy to see us? Two girls that love hanging out and watching football?"

"I hate football."

Lila glares at me. "We're going. End of subject. It's Friday—what're you doing tonight?"

I exhale and shred Lila's napkin. She can be so bossy sometimes. "Babysitting."

"For who, Camille?"

"Ha-ha, you're a real comedian," I say. It's not really funny, though. My mom *has* specifically asked me to stay home and hang out with Camille before. "For a fifth-grader in my carpool."

"Ah, fun."

"Yes, mucho fun. But I need the cash. What are *you* doing?"

"Absolutely nothing," she admits. "We really need to get on the guy circuit. Which is why we're going to the football game tomorrow. This is the answer, I promise."

"Great." I gather my books to head to first period. "Looking forward to it. Football. Woo-hoo."

--- --- --- ---

During French class, I deliberately sit by Isabelle. I don't say hi or anything, I just slip into the seat behind her instead of my usual one by the window. It's funny how I've hardly thought about her all year and today I've been seeing her everywhere— in the hallways, in the library, at the soda machine.

Madame asks us to practice some *Conversation* passages from our textbook with a partner and correct each other's pronunciation. She pairs everyone up around the room, and since I'm behind Isabelle, we get put together.

"Hey," I say to her when she turns around. She looks slightly surprised to see me sitting there, and I wonder if she'll mention our meeting yesterday. "What page?"

"Eighty-four," Isabelle replies, her face in her book. "*Ce pain semble délicieux. Prenez-vous du beurre?*" *This bread looks delicious. Do you have any butter?* Her pronunciation is excellent.

"*Non, le beurre est haut en graisse,*" I reply. "*Il vous donnera de grandes cuisses.*" No, butter is high in fat. It'll give you big thighs.

Isabelle wrinkles her brow. "That's not what it says. Are you on page eighty-four?"

My ears turn red. "I'm just kidding."

"Is it on the next page?"

I sigh. "No, it's a *joke.*" Isabelle is still scanning the page. I start to get embarrassed, hoping she won't realize I was showing off for her. "Never mind," I say. "*Voici le beurre. Voulez-vous la gelée?*"

I stick like glue to the rest of the passage until Madame calls our attention to the board. Isabelle turns her back to me and we go on with class. She's not chilly or anything, but she's not particularly friendly, either. I wonder if that's what our relationship is, or if she didn't like that I met Epp while she was away.

I take notes and try to pay attention, but a mean little part of me wonders why I never noticed before that Isabelle's missing a sense of humor. An even meaner part of me wonders how soon Epp will figure it out.

— — — —

Mom and Camille come into my room as I'm getting ready for babysitting.

"Hi, chicky," Mom says. "How was your day?"

"Fine," I say, looking around frantically for my hairbrush. I always lose things when I'm in a hurry. "I walked Camille at four; she peed and pooped."

"That's good, but I was asking about *you.*"

"The usual—class, class, class, homework, homework, homework." I find my brush under the bed, where Camille must have dragged it to chew on the handle, and pull it through my hair.

"Any fun plans this weekend?"

"Besides babysitting tonight?" I joke. "Well, Lila wants me to go to a football game at St. Ivan's with her tomorrow. Can you give us a ride around twelve thirty?"

"Football? You've never been interested in football before."

"I'm not interested now. Lila is. Can you give us a ride?"

She nods. "Of course. I'm not sure it'll be a very nice day for sitting outside, but—"

"What about you?" I cut in before she launches into a lecture about dressing properly for cold weather. "What are your 'fun plans' this weekend?"

"Well, Camille and I are going to make a big pot of chili. And I need to get a gift for a woman at work who had a baby."

I pull my hair into a ponytail and zip on a hoodie. "C'mon, Mom. You should go out. Call a friend. One with *two* legs."

"I've told you, Taryn, I can manage my own social life." Her voice is just the tiniest bit sharp. "And I like it the way it is right now."

"All I'm saying is you should get out a little more."

"*Taryn.*" Her voice passes sharp and goes right to angry.

A horn honks outside. "That's my ride," I say, glad to be interrupted. I didn't mean to make her mad; I know she knows my dad has been seeing someone. "I should be home around midnight."

"All right. Call me if you need anything."

Chapter Four

When Lila and I arrive at the football game the next day, we scan the crowd and try to figure out where to sit. It's pretty obvious where the home team is, since most of them are wearing navy-and-gold St. Ivan's sweatshirts. A bunch have even painted their faces blue. They look kind of stupid to me, since this is just a high school game, but I don't even go to games at my own school, so what do I know?

Lila's wearing a tight V-neck sweater and looks pretty hot. I wish she looked a little less hot, since I have enough competition from Isabelle, but I couldn't ask her to ugly it up for the game. She plans to meet her dream guy today. I'm wearing another flattering sweater-and-scarf ensemble and my super-fitted jeans.

I look for Epp, but in a sea of several hundred guys, most of them with dark hair, he isn't easy to spot.

Lila pushes her way up the side of the bleachers and

wriggles down a middle row. "Taryn!" she snaps at me. "C'mon!"

I'm staring nervously at the crowd, overwhelmed by the sight of so many teenage guys. There are very few girls in the stands. "Okay, okay."

I follow her and we squeeze into an empty space. I glance at the scoreboard and see that St. Ivan's is ahead by one point. The guys sitting around us are a sea of energy: cheering, growling, and yelling at the game. Most of them have their hoods up because of the cold and they stamp their feet on the bleachers instead of clapping. It's very raw, very caveman, and completely different from our polite, civilized girls' school.

Lila and I sit quietly, observing. Everything the guys around us say is said in the loudest voice possible, as if they are hoping people on Mars will hear it. They stand up when certain things happen on the field, and yell rude chants at the other team. I wonder how girls manage to concentrate at coed schools.

It's so cold I have to sit on my gloved hands to keep them warm. I remind myself that I voluntarily agreed to come and sit outside on a Saturday in December so I could maybe run into a guy who already has a girlfriend.

"Do you see him?" Lila whispers. The whispering is unnecessary. Everyone but us is yelling at the game.

"Nope—all I see are the backs of people's heads. Maybe this wasn't a good idea."

"Of course it was a good idea," Lila insists. "We're *in* it."

"In what?"

"In *it*. The thick of it. I don't know. But we're in it."

Thank goodness one of us is enjoying herself. Lila even has her coat unzipped so her cute sweater shows.

"I'm going to get some hot cider," I say. "Want some?" She nods, and I push my way back along the length of the bleacher and down the steps. Despite my jeans, no one pays any attention to me. How can all of these boys be so interested in football? They go to an all-boys school. Shouldn't they be the tiniest bit excited to see a girl?

I decide to find a bathroom before getting the cider. Something about these jeans seems to decrease the size of my bladder.

In the gymnasium next to the field, I see a sign for restrooms. I lock myself in a stall and a minute later feel much better. As I'm adjusting my sweater, I hear several girls come into the bathroom.

"Of course we're going to his Christmas dance," says a voice I immediately recognize. It's Isabelle. She has a weird way of overpronouncing words, so that "Christmas" sounds like "chrisss-TUH-mussss." "It's on the twenty-second, the day after break starts."

"What're you going to wear?" one of her friends asks, sounding homicidally envious. Going to the St. Ivan's Christmas dance is a big deal, even I know that. It's usually held somewhere fancy downtown by the Inner Harbor. All the other schools have theirs in the gym.

"A sleeveless black silk dress that's cut really low in the front. It has a sparkly brooch right between my boobs." Isabelle laughs. "Epp'll *love* it."

I gag quietly. Then I realize the predicament I'm in. I can't stay in the stall forever; they'll notice there are feet below the door. So I push my shoulders back, unlock the door, and walk semiconfidently over to the sink to wash my hands.

Isabelle catches my reflection in the mirror where she's brushing her hair. "Hey, Taryn," she says. "I didn't know you were dating a St. Ivan's guy."

I try to keep from smacking her. Isabelle knows I'm not dating a St. Ivan's guy, because if I were, she would have heard about it. And since only girlfriends and desperate single girls come to games, she's just called me a loser.

She and her friends stare at me, waiting for a response. Where is Lila when I need her? I'm outnumbered. "I'm not—I mean, I'm here for the school paper." I bite my tongue as soon as the sentence is out. What a stupid lie.

Isabelle tilts her head. "Why is the *Mighty Quill* covering a St. Ivan's game?"

"Well," I continue, feeling my face get red, "I'm writing an article on how guys' sports are different than girls' sports."

Isabelle nods thoughtfully. "That's interesting. Are you interviewing people?"

"Yeah, sure. A couple of interviews." I'm making this up as I go, hoping Isabelle's friends don't know I'm not on the paper.

One of the girls, who looks like a blond bunny rabbit and is a junior at Eastley, nudges Isabelle. They exchange a look I don't understand.

"You know," Isabelle says, "my booooooyyfrrrriennnnd goes here. And he's on the lacrosse and track teams."

Epp plays lacrosse and runs track! A butterfly flutters in my stomach—I've found out something new about him.

"He'd be perfect for your interview," she says.

I grip the slimy bathroom counter to keep from jumping up and down and revealing how ecstatic I am. Isabelle has just handed me the perfect opportunity to get to know Epp. To talk to him again, ask him questions about himself. It would almost be like a date.

"I guess that could work," I say cautiously. I'm a bad liar, so the idea of pretending to be on the paper is completely insane. But I can't help myself. "When should we do it?"

"Do you have your questions with you?" Bunny Rabbit asks.

"Questions?"

"You know," she says, "to ask him for the article."

Oops. "Yeah, yeah, I have my questions." I pat my jeans pocket, which has a twenty-dollar bill tucked inside and no questions whatsoever.

"Then let's go." Isabelle beckons her troops and me to follow and we leave the restroom.

As we march up the bleachers, I glance over at Lila and see she's been watching me walk with Isabelle around the perimeter of the field. She tries to mouth something to me, but I can't figure out what it is. I shrug at her and keep going.

Isabelle climbs to the topmost bleacher and scoots along the row. A bunch of guys see her coming and stand up to let her pass, not even caring that their team is trying for a field goal and they can't see it. A few of them glance at her butt as she passes.

Since I'm directly behind her and she's taller than I am, I can't see where we're going. A second later she plops down next to Epp and I practically fall into his lap, which sounds a lot better than it really is, because no one looks good with their arms flailing.

"Hey," he says, catching my wrist.

I straighten up and he lets go. It might be my imagination, but he looks happy to see me.

Isabelle grabs his hand, the one that just touched me, and squeezes it. "Guess what? Taryn's doing a story for our school's paper on guys who play sports and she wants to write the article about you!"

What is she talking about? That is *not* the lie I told in the bathroom. I said something else entirely, something like girls' sports versus boys'. It's hard to remember now. Epp's wearing his varsity track jacket and his nose and cheeks are pink from the cold.

I realize if I don't tell Epp that including him in the article was Isabelle's idea, he might assume, correctly, that I'm stalking him.

"Actually," I say, sounding a lot more confident than I feel, "Isabelle mentioned you might want to be in the article after I told her what I was working on. But if you don't want to, I completely understand . . . "

Epp's ears redden. He glances at Isabelle, like he's uncertain what's going on. "You want me to be in your school's newspaper?" he asks her.

"Sure, why not?" she says. "You'll just be talking about track and lacrosse."

Several rows down and to my right, I catch a glimpse of Lila. She's completely turned around in her seat and watching our little scene. She looks impressed. I went off for cider and now I'm talking with Epp like we're best buds.

"What's your name again?" I ask, stalling for time.

Epp squints at me. "John Epplin." He says it very clearly, like I might be a little slow. It's the third time we've met, so you can hardly blame him for wondering why I can't remember his name. "Can we do the interview now?"

I think fast. The lies are getting bigger every second. "I'm supposed to be observing the game right now. That's a big part of the article."

Isabelle says, "If you can't do it today, you should set up a time to meet after school one day this week. I'm sure Taryn has a deadline."

"Okay," Epp says. "Where should we do it?"

"My house," Isabelle suggests. "Taryn lives right near me."

"No! I m-mean, uhh . . . " I stammer. If I'm going to go to the trouble of doing a fake interview, I'd better get to be alone with him. "I'm supposed to conduct interviews at the interviewee's school."

"I don't have practice Tuesday," Epp says. "Want to meet over by the gym doors?"

"I can't come Tuesday!" Isabelle moans. "The Medleys are singing at a senior center." The Medleys are our school's a cappella singing group. The group is audition-only, and made up of the sixteen best singers in the school. I'm not even in the Glee Club, which anyone can join.

"Tuesday's good for me," I say quickly. Isabelle frowns, but Epp smiles and doesn't seem the least bit bothered that Isabelle can't make it.

"Well, I guess I'd better go take notes on the game," I say. "I'll see you Tuesday." I turn around and squeeze down the row of bleachers again. When I finally get back to where Lila's waiting, I collapse in my seat. Despite the cold, I'm hot and sweaty, like I've just run laps.

"What happened?" Lila shrieks. "What were you doing up there? I've been dying!"

"*You've* been dying?" I fill her in on how, with one trip to the bathroom, I've suddenly become a star reporter for the *Mighty Quill.*

Lila gapes at me like a fish. "Don't tell me," I say. "I know—I'm so stupid. My mom always says when you tell one little lie, it snowballs into something else. And that's exactly what happened."

"That's not what I was going to say," Lila replies. "I was going to say I think it's brilliant."

"*Brilliant?* To have a fake interview for a fake article? It's a nightmare!"

"It's *brilliant.* You meet with him, ask for his phone number or email to check facts with him later, write the article, send it to him, et cetera. You guys'll have to keep talking. You'll be engaged by the time it's over!" She claps her hands with glee.

Lila's a supportive friend, I have to give her that. Deranged, but supportive.

"But how can I pretend I'm on the paper? Isabelle knows everybody at Eastley. She'll find out!" I put my head in my hands. Now that I'm not standing next to Epp, basking in his beauty, the total stupidity of what I've done hits me.

"We'll think of something. Don't worry about that."

"Okay then, what about the girlfriend problem?" I ask. "It's not like Isabelle's going to spontaneously combust."

"Pfhhhfff," Lila says. "They'll break up in no time. High school relationships are notoriously short." She sees the crushed look on my face and quickly corrects herself. "Except for *your* future relationship with Epp. That'll be forever."

"Thank you."

"You're welcome." Lila pats my knee. "So, did you happen to notice if he had a friend for me?"

Chapter Five

After two sleepless nights and three panicked phone calls to Lila, I decide I have to ask the editor of the *Mighty Quill* if I can write the article for real, even if it means I have to join the paper for the rest of the year. It's much better than being found out, which I eventually would be, since Isabelle is bound to say something to someone on the paper.

So during my free period on Monday, I head up to the *Quill*'s office, which is in an old storage room tucked away on the top floor of the school. I've never been in it before, and I'm surprised by how cramped it is. It's dark and windowless, with three desks jammed inside, a few computers, and a giant printer with a stack of recycled paper next to it. The far wall is completely obscured by empty soda cans stacked like bricks.

There's only one person in there at the moment, a girl with straight dark hair and a pretty face, hidden by black plastic-framed glasses.

"Hi," I say, stepping inside. "I'm Taryn Greenleaf. I have an idea for an article?" I try to sound confident, but my voice just comes out loud.

"I'm Carla Wooden, the editor," the girl says, peering up at me through her glasses. "What's your idea?"

I recite the line I rehearsed. "Well, I'd like to interview some athletes from Eastley, and a few guys from a boys' school, and see what they think the differences between boys' and girls' sports are."

"Hmm." Carla chews her lip, thinking it over. "What's your hypothesis?"

"My what?"

Carla smiles—a tight, severe smile. "Your theory. What are you hoping to prove with the article?"

This is harder than I thought. "That, uh, well, I don't know yet. I went to a game at St. Ivan's this weekend and the atmosphere was so different from what it's like at our games. I just thought it might be interesting."

She chews her lip some more. "Well, I like that you want to interview students from other schools—we don't usually do that. But I'm afraid we don't let non-staff members write."

My stomach sinks. Isabelle will find out I'm a big fat liar, and I'll be ruined.

"You see," Carla goes on, "if I let non-staff members write, then lots of people would want to write one article to see their byline, but would never help us with edit and layout. They'd get the perk of working on the paper without having to do any of the grunt work."

"I'll do grunt work," I say immediately. I even mean it. I'll do whatever it takes to keep from being found out. "I'd love to join the paper. I just didn't know I could join so late in the year."

"Sure you can. Especially since we're short-staffed this year. I have to warn you, though, it's a lot of work. And I don't like to be let down by my reporters." She gives me a hard stare that tells me she's not kidding.

Despite her stare, relief begins to tingle in my toes. I'm joining the paper. "No problem. I won't let you down."

"Good. How about you come to our meeting today to hear what everyone's working on, and we'll assign you a deadline?" she suggests.

"Sure," I say. "When's the meeting?"

"After last period. Don't be late." Carla hands me a pen. It's red and yellow, our school colors, and says the *Mighty Quill* on it. "Welcome to the *Quill*."

I can't answer a single question I'm asked in my afternoon classes. A massive stress zit has sprouted on my chin, and I'm so busy worrying about the paper and this stupid article that I can barely function. I even blow a pop quiz in English, which I'm normally good at.

When I finally make it upstairs after last period, the *Quill*'s meeting has already begun. Outside the office door, girls sit cross-legged along both sides of the hallway, as if they have a large, invisible table between them. I guess there's no way they can all fit in that tiny office. I inch over to one end and glance at Carla. She's at the head of the invisible table. She motions for me to sit down.

"Everybody," Carla calls out, "this is Taryn. She's just joined the paper, and she'll be doing a special feature about how high school athletes, boys and girls, perceive themselves and are perceived by others."

Whoa. That sounds really ambitious coming out of her mouth. And nothing at all like what I'd told her I was writing about.

"Hi," I say tentatively. The girls turn their heads to check me out. Four of them are wearing black-framed glasses like Carla.

She brings the meeting to order, which mostly consists of her listing stories they need to work on, assigning jobs to people, and reminding everyone to keep the office clean. "Stop leaving food around," Carla warns. "We don't want to lose eating privileges in the office. And somebody better throw out that orange peel—I'm not touching it."

Heads bob up and down. I wonder how Carla can be so grossed out by an orange peel when there are hundreds of empty soda cans stacked in the office.

"And quit using the *Quill*'s computers to do homework," Carla continues. "Go to the computer lab like everybody else. All articles for the next issue are due in two weeks. No exceptions. Questions?"

Total silence. I get the feeling Carla is a sort of a dictator. A likable dictator, but a dictator nonetheless.

"Dismissed," Carla says. "And Taryn, I want to see a rough draft of your article at next Monday's meeting."

— — — —

I call my mom as soon as I'm out of the meeting, and she and Camille come pick me up.

"Hello, chicky," Mom says as I climb into the car. She honks loudly as someone cuts in front of us. I glance over, and as luck would have it, it's my English teacher, probably hurrying home to grade my pop quiz. "Why'd you miss carpool?"

"I was at a meeting for the school paper." Camille gives me a vigorous all-over sniffing as I climb into the car. *You smell like gym class*, her eyes say. "Move it, Camille," I say, pushing her away.

"Really?" Mom taps the brakes and Camille gets jerked into the steering wheel climbing back into Mom's lap. "Have you decided to join?"

"Yeah. My first article will be in the next issue."

"Taryn, that's great!" Mom sounds so excited you'd think I'd won the lottery. "That'll look terrific on your college applications."

"That's why I did it," I reply, looking out the window so she can't see the face I'm making. "For college."

"Good for you, chicky. That's the spirit."

I need to change the subject. The lies are making my chin zit throb. "How's work?" I ask.

"Nuts, absolutely nuts. We're knocking down a wall to

make room for four more lawyers, and the bosses can't seem to get it into their heads that I'm just the office manager, I'm not a contractor. I can't tell them why the workers aren't done yet." Mom takes a right where we normally go straight. "Shall we pick up some Chinese for dinner?" she asks casually.

I'm immediately suspicious. I love Chinese takeout, but Mom doesn't think it's healthy, so she only gets it when she has a motive. "Whatever it is, just tell me, Mom."

"Tell you what?" She looks over at me and back at the road. "Fine. Your dad called today and wants to know if you're staying with me for all of Christmas break."

"I thought that was in the contract."

"It's not a contract, Taryn—it's shared custody. And yes, technically you're supposed to stay with me, since you spent Thanksgiving with him, but if you want to go for a few days, that's fine."

I can hear in her voice that it isn't fine, but she doesn't want to say no. "I don't know," I say.

"Well, think about it then. But I told him you'd let him know yourself, okay? I don't want to be in the middle of you two making plans."

"That's funny. I thought I was in the middle."

"Ha-ha." Mom pulls into a spot at the Chinese restaurant and parks. "You stay here with Camille, and I'll run in and get some chow mein. Want anything else?"

I shake my head and look out the window. "Nope."

Lila calls and I fill her in on my talk with Carla and details from the *Quill* meeting.

"Those girls are scary," I tell her. "They're so serious about the paper. And I've never written anything but English essays!"

"Piece of cake," Lila says. "You're already through the toughest part—you're officially on the paper. You have a press pass. That means *total access.* You can tell Epp you need to go to his house and see his room for the article. Or ask him if he prefers boxers or briefs. Or blondes or brunettes."

"He prefers redheads," I say bitterly. "That's pretty clear."

"C'mon, Taryn. This is progress. And your interview's tomorrow—let's start prepping you."

"Aren't I going too far though?" I ask. "I mean, I think Epp is awesome, and I'd love to have him dump Isabelle and take me to his Christmas dance instead. But it's not going to happen. So why am I putting myself through this? I should be studying Latin declensions."

Lila snorts. "Look at this as a learning experience. You're going to practice talking to a guy, getting to know him. This is valuable stuff—stuff they don't teach at Eastley. You can study Latin when you're dead."

"I think the saying is 'you can sleep when you're dead.'"

"Whatever. Let's focus. You're meeting with Epp tomorrow, and we need to make sure you know what you're doing."

She talks forever, discussing everything from my outfit, to the questions I'll ask, to my body positioning. "Body language speaks volumes," she says. "*Vol*umes. Always cross your legs toward him. Play with your hair."

"Maybe you should be the one doing this," I suggest. "You sure know a lot about guys for someone who's never had a boyfriend."

Lila's quiet for a second, and I realize I sounded mean when I meant to be funny. "I'm just trying to help," she says finally.

"I know, I know. I'm sorry—really. I'm just cranky because I'm nervous."

"Okay." She still sounds hurt. "Well, go to bed. Beauty sleep is important."

"Very," I agree sarcastically. I'd need about twenty years of it to look like Isabelle. "Good night."

Chapter Six

Carpool drops me home after school the next day, and I tear up to my room, pulling off my uniform as I go. I have thirty minutes to change, curl my hair, apply makeup, and bike to St. Ivan's to meet Epp.

Luckily, Lila chose my outfit last night: a white V-neck T-shirt and a super-small argyle cardigan. The cardigan started out normal-size, but then I washed it and it shrunk. It turns out it fits me better shrunken, and the busy pattern makes my chest look bigger. I'm wearing my fitted leather jacket again, because it's not very warm and will keep me from sweating too much while I bike. I put on a looser pair of jeans, because the last thing I need during the interview is a big rip in the butt cheek from pedaling.

After primping, glossing, curling, brushing, and gargling, I'm ready. There's just one little problem—Mom isn't home yet—which means Camille won't get a walk until she arrives. I don't have time to take her out, but if

Mom comes home and finds a mess on the rug, I'm dead.

I decide to have a talk with Camille, sister to sister. I yell for her and find her sitting impatiently by the back door, her paw scratch, scratch, scratching.

"Camille," I say, "listen up. I'm going to meet a guy right now, and I really like him. You met him the other day, remember? And I need to leave *right now* so I can bike over to St. Ivan's slowly and not get sweaty. So I can't take you out. But Mom will be home any minute and she'll take you for a nice walk. I'll even leave her a note. Okay?"

Camille sniffs at my shoe, then steps on it with her paw. Her black eyes peer up at me hopefully. *I've been alone all day. I would really like to pee. And maybe some play time. Take me out!*

"Can't do it, Camille. But I promise to make up for it later. I *swear.*"

Her gaze grows more intense and a whine comes from deep in her furry throat. *I really, really need to go out. Take me, or you'll be sorry!*

I ponder this for a minute. Camille could definitely inflict damage on my personal belongings. Not to mention poop in places I don't want to think about. "Fine," I say. "A two-minute pee, Camille. That's it."

Nine minutes later, because Camille would not be hurried, I'm on my bike heading toward St. Ivan's. It's hard to remember to go slowly when my heart is beating so hard I can feel it in my throat. My armpits are becoming the slightest bit damp.

I coast through the school entrance and slide my bike into

the bike rack. I don't see anyone nearby, so I give my T-zone a quick swipe of pressed powder. I glance in my tiny compact mirror and am happy to see that aside from my angry chin zit, I look semidecent. I whip out a steno book and my *Mighty Quill* pen, hoping I look authentic.

I walk to the gym doors, paranoid a teacher will stop me and ask what I'm doing walking around on a boys' campus. Guys are strolling by in twos and threes, their blazers hanging open and their ties stuffed into their pockets. They glance at me curiously as they go by. Even though it's probably thirty-five degrees out, none of them wear winter coats.

Epp is waiting on a bench for me, wearing a dark green corduroy blazer and khakis. He's still got his tie on but the knot is pulled down to the middle of his chest. I'm suddenly self-conscious about my makeup and curled hair. Maybe I should have just worn my uniform. After all, no matter what I do to myself, I won't look like Isabelle.

I clear my throat to keep my voice from getting watery. "Hey—ready for the interview?"

"Hope so." He smiles up at me. Everything about him is just right. Even his eyebrows, which are a little darker than his hair and make his eyes stand out.

"Where should we . . . ," I say. "I mean, do you want to sit here? Or go somewhere else?"

"Here's fine. Unless you think you'll get cold."

I'm already cold, but I don't want to be a wuss. So I sit down on the bench beside him, not too close, but not too far that it looks like I'm trying to sit far away from him. We're looking out over the empty football field and bleachers. We can't see the rest of campus or anyone walking by. We're completely alone, like the snow day.

"You didn't bring Camille," he says. "Doesn't she like interviews?"

"She doesn't like anything, including me." I blush. Why did I say that?

He looks confused. "Why doesn't she like you? She's your dog, isn't she?"

"No, she's really my mom's dog. Mom takes her everywhere, lets her sleep in her bed, cooks her special food. My dad moved out two years ago, and we got Camille right after, partly because the house felt so empty, and . . . " I let my voice trail off. I don't want to tell him my dad had never wanted a dog and my mom did it to spite him. "Anyway, my mom said the dog was for me, but really she's her baby."

"I get it," Epp says. "And you want Camille to be yours."

"No, well, sort of. It's more like I wish my mom had something in her life other than just Camille." I can't believe I'm talking about this with him, like it's a normal conversation to be having with an almost stranger. "I'm sorry, I know this is too much information."

"No problem. It's okay to be worried about your mom, you know."

I smile at him gratefully and our eyes lock for a second. It feels really intimate, like a hug, even though we're sitting two feet away from each other.

"Well, we should probably start the interview," I say hastily, looking down at my notebook. I'm talking too much. I doubt Isabelle bores him with her family problems.

"Fire away." Epp drums his heels on the cement.

It's getting colder by the minute, and I can see my breath in the air. The lights have come on in the football stadium and they twinkle like stars on the dark field in front of us. I can't remember any of my warm-up questions. Lila told me to write them down but I didn't listen. I throw out the only question I can think of. "What's your favorite color?"

He laughs. "Really? That's a real question?"

"Yes," I say defensively. "Lots of reporters use it."

"Okay. Uh, blue. Dark blue."

I write down *blue*, like it's very important. "Are you a vegetarian?"

Epp shakes his head. "No. I eat everything."

"What's your sign?" I'm making these up as I go.

Epp thinks a minute. "I don't know. What's August?"

"I think it's Leo."

"Well, then, Leo." He pauses. "Is that going to be in the article?"

"No, those were just to warm up. We'll do the real questions now ... " I flip to the page in my notebook where I wrote down the questions for the interview. I'm pretty sure a real reporter would not be acting like I am, asking stupid questions like his favorite color and telling him about my parents' divorce.

I skim the page and clear my throat again. "So, you run track and play lacrosse. Which is your favorite?"

"Track."

"Really? I thought you'd say lacrosse."

"Lacrosse gets a lot more attention, especially around here, but track is more challenging."

"What first attracted you to track?"

"I've always been fast," he says. "And I like to run hard. So it seemed like a good fit."

I write hurriedly, trying to copy every word. "What's your race?"

"Four hundred–meter hurdles."

"Hurdles . . . and why do you run that particular race?"

He shrugs. "Because I'm not fast enough to run the four hundred and I'm too fast for the eight hundred. And my coach says I have heart. You've got to have heart to run the four hundred–meter hurdles."

I don't totally understand what he's talking about, but I jot it all down. "What's the hardest thing about running track?"

"The training, I guess. I've played a lot of sports, and no sport other than maybe swimming has harder workouts. There's something really satisfying about pushing yourself every single day to do better than you did the day before. And track is all about improving by seconds, which seem so minuscule, but in track you win or lose by fractions of a second."

My hand is cramping up from my frantic note taking. I'm getting a different picture of Epp than the one I had before. I'd thought he was just a hot, popular jock. But he's also hardworking. And determined. And he listened to me when I spilled my guts to him. "Do you think track gets less attention than lacrosse at your school?"

"Of course it gets less attention," he says, laughing. "What do you think is more fun, watching a lacrosse game or a sprint?"

"Touché." We grin at each other. "Is it hard to play two sports and keep your GPA up?"

"Nah, I think it helps me organize my time better. Doesn't working on the paper do the same for you?"

I hesitate, not wanting to tell more lies about the paper. "I guess so. I'm pretty organized, though. My notebooks for each class are color-coordinated to match their textbooks."

Epp laughs again and I feel a spark of electricity between us. An honest-to-goodness spark.

"So, what do you think of female athletes?" This is Lila's question, of course.

"I love them," he replies, smiling. "Nothing better than a hardworking female athlete."

Isabelle plays tennis. Ugh. "How about hardworking female reporters?" I ask.

"They're nice too. But you don't see them running around in shorts much."

Oh, great. He's picturing Isabelle's legs, which are considerably nicer than mine. "How fast can you run a mile?"

"Just under six minutes."

I go on with my prepared questions about training, the lacrosse team, and how he thinks athletes are viewed at St. Ivan's. When I've finally run through all of my questions, it's gotten so dark it's difficult to write. I didn't think about how dark it would be at five o'clock, and I still need to ride my bike home.

"Well, I guess that's all I need, " I say reluctantly. Then, remembering Lila's advice, I add, "Can I get your email address? In case I have any follow-up questions?"

"Sure, it's *jepplin@stivans.edu*. I've got to getting going, too. I've got Driver's Ed tonight."

My heart twitches. "I'm taking it too. Which classes do you have left?"

"Tonight's my last one and then I can get my license. I'm already sixteen." I try to hide my disappointment. There's no chance I'll run into him there now. "You have a ride, right?" Epp asks, standing up. "Can I walk you somewhere?"

I cannot allow Epp to walk me to my bike when he's about to get his license. That would be too, too humiliating. "I've got a ride," I tell him. "I'm going to sit here for a minute and organize my notes."

"Okay, see you soon then," he says. "Can't wait to read the article."

Our eyes meet one last time and he takes off across campus. I sit with my pen in my hand, watching him walk away and feeling my breath cold in my chest.

                     — — — —

At home I'm greeted by the warm welcome of my mother being very angry with me.

"Taryn, is there something you want to tell me?" Mom's standing in the family room with her arms crossed. Camille hides behind her left leg, not looking at me.

My buzz from the interview evaporates. "Like what?"

"Like that you cheated Camille out of her favorite part of the day—her long walk with you?"

How on earth did Camille tell her we only went out for a pee? "I took her out, Mom. But I had to hurry because I had an interview for the paper." I hold up my steno pad and *Mighty Quill* pen to corroborate my story.

Mom looks down at the dog, then at me. "Taryn, Camille relies on you. *I* rely on you."

This is exactly what I was telling Epp about—my mom's life completely revolves around the dog. Not me, her real daughter. The *dog*.

"When I got home," Mom says, "she was standing at the back door, whining and scratching. It was pitiful."

"I'm *sorry*."

Mom uncrosses her arms and fiddles with the back of a chair. "Did you call your father yet?"

I look away. This is what she's really upset about. "No."

"Well, have you decided whether you're going to visit him or not? Because you'll need to take your books if you go. Your exams are right after Christmas."

I grit my teeth to keep from snapping at her. "I know when my exams are."

"Don't leave him hanging, Taryn. Call him and let him know soon, okay?"

"Can I go to my room now?" I scoop up my backpack from the floor. "I want to write up my notes from the interview."

"Yes. Dinner's in an hour."

"Okay."

"And you need to set the table."

"*Okay.*"

— — — —

Alone in my room, I change into boxers and a sweatshirt. I glance in the mirror and compare myself with Isabelle. My legs are winter white, and since I've been wearing tights to school every day, I haven't shaved for over a week. My legs are pale and hairy. Reporter legs. Not tennis-star legs.

Camille pushes open my door with her nose and wanders into my room. She checks out my legs, too.

"What do you think of my legs, Camille? They're white and hairy, like yours. Ha!" I laugh at my joke.

Camille turns up her nose at me. *It's good you have a sense of humor about it.*

"I'm sorry about the short walk earlier. I told you I was in a hurry."

Her expression becomes smug. *It's okay. Mom took me out and then we snuggled on the couch.*

"I know; you're Mommy's little girl. Don't remind me." I bend over and scratch her under her chin, just where she likes to be scratched. "You're a pain, Camille. But part of me is glad Mom has you to hang out with."

Camille gives me a doggy grin and jumps up on my bed. I climb up next to her with my books, and she curls around my feet to keep me company while I start my homework.

Sometimes, although it's very rare, I really like my dog.

Chapter Seven

Lila passes me a note in Latin class. *I figured out how you can get to know Epp better . . .*

I spent all last night replaying my interview with him in my mind. How he looked, what he said, how easy he was to talk to. One meeting with him wasn't enough—I need more. Nervous, but intrigued, I write a big ? on her note and pass it back to her.

Interview Isabelle for the article too. You can find out all about him! And what their relationship is like! It's perfect!

What? Is she crazy? I shake my head at her, but she's looking at the board, pretending to take notes. *I don't want to interview her! I don't even want to talk to her!*

Lila writes something and underlines it three times. *It's perfect and you know it.*

Interviewing Epp was one thing, but Isabelle? There's no way I could do that with a straight face. We may not be friends, but we've known each other forever. *NO WAY,* I write back.

I see her squirm at her desk and it takes her a few minutes to reply. *Don't get mad . . . but I talked to her in American Studies and said you wanted to put her in the article. She said to come to her house after school today.*

I read the note and feel myself getting worked up. What's with Lila lately? It's like she's lost her mind or something. I'm too angry to write a reply, so I crumple the paper and shove it into my backpack. I refuse to look at her for the rest of the period.

After class, she follows me to my locker, looking half-pleased with herself, half-apologetic.

"I can't believe you did that without asking me!" I hiss. I want to yell at her but there are too many people in the halls.

"I know, I'm sooorrrrry," she says, not sounding at all guilt-ridden. "I just know that you and Epp would be perfect together and I want to help."

"You haven't even met him."

"But it's *fate*, Taryn. The way you guys met, him being at the same Driver's Ed class. We should go again this week. Even if Isabelle is there, too."

"There's no point going now. He finished his classes." I fiddle with my locker door and take a deep breath. "I just wish you'd stop pushing so much with all the guy stuff."

She frowns. "It's not going to happen unless we make it happen. That's why I told Isabelle you'd interview her—I know this is the next step for you and Epp."

"*Lila*. You're forcing me to interview her, and I don't even like being around her! And what if she gets suspicious?"

"Relax. This is Isabelle we're talking about, not Sherlock Holmes. I'm sure she believes that she and her boyfriend are important enough to deserve their own newspaper article."

"You'd better hope so." I pull some books out of my locker and slam it shut. Lila blocks my way. "Move—I've got a quiz next period."

She hangs her head a little. "Don't be mad at me, okay? Just do the interview and you'll see I'm right."

"You're not right." I glare at her and head down the hall toward my next class.

I spend my free period revising the questions I asked Epp so they'll work for Isabelle. I cut a bunch of them, because I don't really care what her answers are, and I don't want to be there too long. I just want to do the interview well enough to avoid looking like an idiot.

Rather than taking Camille for another quickie pee and potentially getting busted by my mother again, I decide to take her with me. After all, Isabelle has a dog, and her dog seemed to like Camille. And maybe a little part of me has been feeling guilty for giving her such a short walk yesterday when I know she's home all alone every day.

"Camille, we're going on a walk and visiting my enemy, Isabelle, okay?" I tell her. "She has a dachshund. You have to be on your best, best behavior, though."

Camille runs in circles by the back door making strangled bird chirp noises in her throat to let me know she'll behave. I Velcro her into her blue parka and grab my backpack. As we trot up the street, I run over the interview questions in my head and remind myself this isn't a big deal. There's no reason to be nervous about interviewing a girl I've known since before I lost my baby teeth.

Camille and I walk up to Isabelle's front door, which is half-covered by a giant holly wreath. I ring the bell and a minute later Isabelle answers. She's wearing jeans and an Eastley Tennis T-shirt, and her feet are bare. Her toenails are painted a dark, sexy maroon, and her reddish hair is tied into a loose braid. I feel stupid still being in my uniform when she looks so casual.

"Hey," she says. "Come on in."

"I hope it's okay that I brought my dog." I gesture at Camille, who's hiding behind my legs. "She's home by herself all day when my mom's at work."

"No problem." Isabelle opens the door and I scoop up Camille so she won't track in any paw prints. She's being surprisingly easygoing. She doesn't even growl at Isabelle.

"Let's talk in my room," Isabelle says, starting up the stairs.

I follow, noticing how nice her house looks. There are potted poinsettias in the foyer, all of the furniture seems new, and the walls look freshly painted. My house has started to look pretty shabby since my dad's been gone.

Mom doesn't know how to fix anything, so if something breaks, it just stays broken.

We go into Isabelle's room, and I'm surprised to see how much it's changed since we were kids. It used to be pink and white, with ponies and dolls everywhere, but now it's painted a bright aqua and the furniture and accessories are straight out of a trendy catalog. There are framed black and white prints on the walls and an overstuffed chair in the corner. A gingerbread-scented candle burns on her desk. It's a very cool room, one you could show your boyfriend, unlike my own room, which hasn't changed much since I was ten.

Camille fidgets so I take off her parka so she won't get too hot. "Can I put her down?" I ask. "She won't chew on anything."

"Sure, go ahead. I'll close my door so Mitzy doesn't come in." Isabelle shuts the door and makes herself a pillow-nest on the bed. She runs her fingers down her long braid, and examines the bottom for split ends. "So, where do we start?"

I plop down on the floor and pull my notebook and *Mighty Quill* pen from my bag. I flip to my questions page and skim them. "What's your favorite color," I say jokingly, remembering the stupid way I began the interview with Epp.

Isabelle squeezes her eyes shut a moment. "Mmm, lavender."

"I was kidding," I say. "But okay." I scrawl *lavender* on my paper.

"Oh!" Isabelle laughs. "Epp told me you asked him that, too, so I figured—"

"He told you that?" I wonder if he was making fun of me, or if it was just a detail he included. And I wonder what else he said.

"We tell each other everything," Isabelle says emphatically. "Like, everything."

This is it—my opportunity to find out more about him. Maybe Lila was right. "That's great you guys talk so much," I gush. "How long have you been going out?"

"Almost four months. He gave me that stuffed polar bear for our three-month anniversary." She points behind me to a three-foot-tall bear wearing a pair of her sunglasses. "He's the best," she goes on. "Really, the best boyfriend I've ever had. He calls me every night, and we hang out every weekend."

Isabelle's cheeks flush and she gazes dreamily at the polar bear. With a sick feeling in my stomach, I realize how much she likes Epp.

Before I have a chance to fully digest Isabelle's happiness, I detect a familiar scent. Camille, my ever-faithful hound, has just peed under the desk. My eyes dart to Isabelle's face. She's wrinkling her nose and looking slightly confused. She turns and looks accusingly at Camille who has run from the scene of the crime and is now sniffing my backpack.

"Did she just . . . ?" Isabelle asks.

I nod, humiliated.

"Oh God, okay—I'll get paper towels." Isabelle jumps up from the bed and runs out of the room.

"*Camille,*" I scold. "You peed outside ten minutes ago!

What is the matter with you?" She looks back at me, but not quite in the eye. She knows she's not allowed to pee in our house. Does she think the rules are different here? Or maybe, just maybe, is she showing me some loyalty by peeing in the house of my enemy?

I scan the room, hoping to find something I can use to sop up the mess. But Isabelle is too neat and tidy to have an old towel lying around. Everything is put away neatly or stacked in kitschy piles. As I search, I notice a picture in a silver frame on top of her dresser. It's Isabelle and Epp sitting on the beach, and she's snuggled up under his arm. The sick feeling in my stomach gets worse.

Isabelle runs in with a spray bottle of pet cleaner and a roll of paper towels. She starts to clean up the mess herself, but I grab the bottle from her. "Stop, Isabelle. She's my dog. And I'm *so sorry*. She never does this at home."

"Don't worry about it." Isabelle shrugs. "She probably smelled Mitzy and wanted to mark her territory."

I always assume that when Camille does anything, it's because of a deliberate and malicious plan. Maybe I give her too much credit sometimes. I look over at her, cuddled up next to the polar bear, her white fur blending in with the bear's. I'm about to give her a forgiving look, when I swear she winks at me.

I knew it.

"Let's start the interview," I say.

"Good idea." Isabelle settles into her pillow-nest again.

"I've got a ton of homework, and Epp's going to call at eight."

My jealousy glows brighter. They have a phone date.

I grab my list and begin rattling off questions about her tennis practices, how long she's been on the team, the pressure she feels before a match, and whether she thinks there's a difference between girls' sports and guys' sports.

"I don't think a girl playing a sport at a girls' school is any different than a guy playing at a guys' school," she says. "The difference would be girls' sports at a co-ed school, because the guys' teams would always take precedence. At Eastley, there are only girls' teams, so everyone roots for the girls."

"You're right! I hadn't thought of that." I quickly write it down, knowing Carla will like it. Not only has Isabelle just helped me with my article, she's also given me the perfect reason to send a follow-up email to Epp—to get his opinion on this new theory. I feel a twinge in my conscience for thinking about Epp while sitting in his girlfriend's bedroom, but I can't help it.

"Do you think you and Epp like each other because you both play sports?" I ask casually.

Isabelle shakes her head, no. "It's one of the things we have in common, but it doesn't have anything to do with our relationship. We like hanging out together."

"Do you ever fight?" Even I'm surprised to hear me ask this. It's so nosey. But I feel compelled to find out every detail about the two of them, even if it's painful to hear.

"No, what would we fight about?" She sounds matter-of-fact, but there's a strain in her voice that wasn't there a second ago, like I'd touched a nerve.

I decide to switch to something safer. "How'd you guys meet?"

Isabelle smiles and looks over at the bear again. "At a party. I went with Lindsey Wexler, you know her?" I nod, but I don't really know her. She's a junior on the tennis team. "It was at her boyfriend's house. We were all hanging out, and Epp sat down next to me and asked how I knew Lindsey, and then we just started talking. And we talked for the rest of the night."

I want to keep asking questions, but Camille comes over and starts nudging my leg. She looks at me deliberately, as if to say, *Can we go? I'm bored.*

"I should go," I say reluctantly. If Camille starts getting antsy she might pee again. Or worse. "But I think I got enough for the interview."

"Oh, good. Thanks for including me. I can't wait to read it! When's it going to run?"

"Um, the next issue."

I pack up my things, including Camille. She stands patiently while I Velcro her into her parka and manages not to pee. "I'm so sorry again about your rug."

"Forget it, really," Isabelle replies. She smiles at Camille. "I like her blue coat. Mitzy would kill me if I tried to put clothes on her."

The phone on her desk rings, playing a pop song instead

of a regular ring. "Hello?" she answers. "Ohhh, hi. I thought you weren't calling till later." Her face goes soft and mushy, like a pink-frosted cupcake.

The sight of her on the phone with him is too much. "I'm going to go," I mouth.

Isabelle waves her fingers at me and snuggles back against her pillows for a long talk.

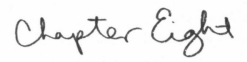

Chapter Eight

After a sleepless night and another morning of faking my way through classes, I know I need help. This Epp thing has gotten out of control.

I find Lila by the cafeteria at noon. "We need to talk," I say, pulling her away from the doors and back into the hallway.

Lila follows, but looks worried. "You're not still mad about yesterday, are you?"

"Sort of, but it doesn't matter, because I need to talk to you. And we can't talk at a lunch table where people might hear us. Let's eat outside."

"But it's winter," Lila protests. "Cold, cold winter. There's no way you're dragging me out there to eat my sandwich."

"Fine—the library."

"We can't eat in the library. If Mrs. Hert smells us, we'll get detention. And she'll definitely smell us, because I have tuna fish."

I scowl. "Oh, excuse me. I thought you were my friend Lila. The one who always has a positive attitude. The one who always has the answer. The one who forced me to interview my enemy yesterday."

Lila swats at my head with her lunch bag. "*Fine*, we'll go wherever you want. Bring on the detention."

She follows me down the hall and into the stairwell. On a whim, I lead her into the auditorium and we sit in the back row. "How's this?" I whisper.

"Creepy," Lila whispers back. The acoustics of the theater make even the smallest sounds reverberate around the room. "So what's your prob?" she asks.

"My *prob* is that I talked to Isabelle yesterday for about an hour and she really likes Epp. Like, *really* likes him. There was a picture of them together in her room and they looked disgustingly happy. And he bought her a stuffed bear."

"So?"

"*So*, she was also really nice to me. She acted like we're friends or something. She even cleaned up Camille's *pee.*"

"You brought Camille to the interview?" Lila grimaces. "You're obsessed with that dog."

I glare at her. "I didn't have a choice."

"Okay, so Isabelle was sweetness and light during the interview. Of course she was! You're putting her and her boyfriend in the school paper."

"It was more than that—she was genuinely nice. And I'm trying to *steal* her boyfriend. I'm already planning to email him follow-up questions." I put my head in my hands. "I can't help it! I can't stop thinking about him! And I know a little part of him likes me. I just know it."

I want to explain to Lila that it's not just that I think Epp might like me a little, or that I like him a lot. It's that I know, deep down, that if he were to *really* like me, something huge in my life would change.

"You know what I think?" Lila says. "You want him, you get him. This is a free society. Free trade. Supply and demand. That's how it works."

"I'm not sure that economic theory applies here."

Lila takes a bite of her tuna sandwich and chews. "Okay, think about it this way. They're not married. They're just dating. And they're young, so it won't last anyway. They don't have children . . . "

"They don't have children?" I forget to keep my voice down and it bounces around the theater.

"Shhh!" Lila hisses. "What's going on? Why do you have the guilts? It's not like you and Isabelle are really friends."

I bite my lip. "I know, but we're not *not* friends. And I don't want to be a bad person. This is something a very bad person would do."

We both chew for a minute: Lila on her tuna, me on my peanut butter. "Here's what you do—stop trying to think of ways to steal him, and just focus on the article."

"Huh? How's that solve anything?"

"Send him the follow-up email, keep the conversation going between you two, but make everything strictly about the article. You'll get to know each other better, and if there's something between you guys, you'll both know it."

For once, Lila's advice sounds reasonable. I'll simply focus on the article, and the article only. Then I won't be a boyfriend stealer, I'll just be the girl Epp suddenly realizes he wants to be with.

"I like it," I announce. Lila smiles, pleased I'm not mad at her anymore. "What do you think will happen, though?" I ask her. "Seriously."

"I think he'll be yours by Christmas."

"Good answer."

———

I take a detour on the way to Latin class and run downstairs to the computer lab. If I'm going to focus on the article, I need to get Epp's opinion on Isabelle's theory. And I don't have much time, because it might take him a day or two to reply and my draft is due to Carla on Monday.

I find my notes from my interview with Epp and open my email. Then I carefully type "jepplin@stivans.edu" into the "To:" field. Just seeing his name on the screen makes the blood rush to my face. I tap my fingers against the keyboard, trying to come up with a good subject line.

From: taryn.greenleaf@eastleyprep.edu

To: jepplin@stivans.edu

Subject: More questions for you . . .

Hi,

Thanks for talking to me Tuesday. I interviewed Isabelle yesterday, and she had a good idea for a different angle for the
article. I'd like to get your opinion. Do you have time to talk
before Sunday (I have a Monday deadline)?

Taryn

I read it over. It's not great, but it is all about the article
and not at all flirty. I even mentioned Isabelle. I have to get
to class, so I hit Send and cross my fingers.

— — — —

My heart is pounding in my ears when I get home from
school, wondering if there will be a reply from him. I blow
past Camille at the back door and run upstairs to the guest
room to boot up the computer.

After several painful minutes, I'm finally online. I suck
in a deep breath and open my school email. There's a mes-
sage from my French teacher about a homework assignment and one from my dad, but no reply from Epp. It's
been only a few hours, so maybe he hasn't even checked his
email yet.

I ignore the French assignment and open my dad's email.

From: jgreenleaf@pacbell.net

To: taryn.greenleaf@eastleyprep.edu

Hi honey,

I called your mom the other day to see if it'd be all right for you to come up here for a few days after Xmas. How long is your break? I can take a few days off and we'll go into the city, have dinner with your grandparents one night, etc. I'd love to see you, but it's up to you, since you were just here for T-giving.

Love,

Dad

I feel a lump in my throat, which I quickly swallow. I really would like to see my dad. I could go for just a few days—Mom would hardly even know I was gone. But as I tell myself this, I know it's about more than being away for a few days. I close the email and flag it to reply to later.

When my inbox refreshes, there's a new email. It's a reply from EPPLIN, JOHN. My breath catches and I click to open it.

Subject: Re: More questions for you . . .

Hey—

I've got practice today and tomorrow. Want to go to a movie with me and Isabelle Saturday night? We can talk about your interview stuff.

Epp

I slide down in my chair like a rag doll. Epp invited me *out with him* on Saturday night. Sure, Isabelle will be there, but if I squint at the email a little, it almost looks like he's asking me out. At the very least, he thinks I'm cool enough to hang out with on a Saturday night, even if it's to talk about a stupid article.

I hit Reply immediately and write:

> Subject: Re: re: More questions for you . . .
> Perfect. See you then.

Chapter Nine

Lila comes over Saturday afternoon to help me get ready for the big night. She's carrying a canvas tote bag and a pink plastic lunchbox.

"What's with the lunch?" I ask as we go upstairs to my room.

"Lunch? This isn't lunch. Use your brain—I thought you were a reporter."

"My brain's exhausted, Lila. I've been plotting and scheming all week, my parents are bugging me about Christmas break, and I need a rest, so just tell me, all right?"

Lila gives me a satisfied smile, like the one Camille has when she gets a treat after not performing a trick. "These are the essentials for your makeover."

"Ooh! Like what?"

"Like the *essentials*." Lila pushes open the door to my room and prepares to work. She throws the tote on my bed and places the pink case on my desk. Then she unlatches it and starts pulling stuff out.

"Are bigger boobs in there?" I ask, peering in.

Lila nods. "Actually, yes, bigger boobs are in here. I brought you a padded bra." She whips it out and throws it on the bed with the tote. It's lacy and beige and ugly.

I pick it up and study it. "Don't you think they'll notice I've somehow developed a chest overnight?"

"Of course not."

I'm doubtful. Very doubtful. "Not even Isabelle?"

"Why would she notice? Do you think she's ever checked out your boobs?"

"I've checked out hers."

"So have I," Lila admits. "Hmm, that's a good point. Let's drop the boobs for now and look at the other stuff I brought."

The desk is covered with more lotions and potions than I've ever seen. "Where did you get all this stuff?"

"From Mary's room. The bra and some of the clothes are hers, so we have to return them."

"Clothes?"

Lila opens the tote she brought and a bunch of tops spill out onto the bed. "You have great jeans, so I figured all you need is a shirt to show off Mary's bra."

"A shirt to show off a bra?" It sounds so pathetic. "Have I really sunk to this level?"

Lila looks matter-of-fact. "Yes."

"Well, you don't have to say it out loud." I throw the padded bra at her and miss.

She grabs my shoulders and sits me on the bed. Then she pulls a facecloth from her box of stuff and wipes off my face.

As crazy as Lila's been lately, I'm glad to have her here. I'm nervous enough about having to be around Epp for an entire evening, but Isabelle's going to be there, too, *and* I have to play Reporter Girl again.

"What are we doing, Dr. Lila?" I ask.

Lila examines my face. "First, I'm going to pluck your brows. Then we'll put on a mask to soak up the oil in your skin so it won't be shiny tonight. Then you're going to try on outfits." The tweezers are already in her hand and aimed at my right eyebrow. "Close your eyes," she says.

"I love you, Lila."

"You should."

"I do."

— — — —

I try on tops in all different colors with all different necklines, trying to find the most flattering one. We finally decide a fitted black V-neck sweater with a chunky beaded necklace would be best, because it's funky and will still look good if I spill anything. Black will also make it less obvious I'm wearing a padded bra, or so Lila tells me.

We put my hair up in some special rollers that make your hair wavy, not curly, and Lila starts filing my nails. I feel like a pampered princess.

Camille wanders in to watch the overhaul. She jumps up on my bed and sniffs all of Mary's and Lila's shirts. She seems to particularly like a pink top that Lila ruled out as being "too cutesy." After she investigates it from top to bottom, probably leaving her nose juice all over it, she pushes my pillow down flat and curls up on it to watch us.

I reach over and scratch behind her ears. She takes one look at my face mask and shies away from my hand.

"Don't be a jerk, Camille," I snap. "I've been really nice to you the last few days, and this is how you behave?"

Camille stares back at me. She doesn't look the least bit chastised. In fact, her expression says, *You look like an idiot.*

Maybe I do look stupid with a mud mask on and curlers in my hair and fake boobs strapped to my chest. I'm pretty sure Isabelle isn't doing this right now. She's probably playing backgammon with the elderly or winning a tennis championship.

When the overhaul is complete and Lila has pronounced me gorgeous, she starts to pack up her things. "I wish I had a hot date tonight," she says with a sigh. "You're going to make Epp fall in love with you, and then you'll forget all about me."

"Fat chance," I say. "I'm focusing on the article, remember? But I promise, once I actually *do* have a hot date, you'll have access to every guy at St. Ivan's."

She sighs again, patting my perfectly tousled waves, and wishes me luck. "Not that you'll need it," she adds.

"No," I agree. "It's not like this evening is going to be tricky or awkward or anything."

"A walk in the park."

"Exactly."

I ask my mom if she'd mind giving me a ride to the movie theater, and she doesn't, but she certainly has a lot of questions. Especially when I tell her I'm going to see *Twin Killer* with Isabelle.

"Taryn, I don't want to sound like a nosy mother, but why are we picking up Isabelle to go see a movie that last week you said was the dumbest-sounding movie of all time?"

"Because she asked me to go, and I said I would."

"And why isn't Lila going?" Mom asks.

"Because she has other plans."

"And since when are you and Isabelle Graham friends?"

"We go to school together, Mother," I say, my voice starting to get high and irritated.

"I realize that. But she lives up the street and we aren't even in the same carpool with her because *you* told *me* you don't like her. And now you're going to the movies together?"

I avoid her eyes. "We have a class together this year. And I interviewed her for my article the other day."

Mom picks up Camille and pulls an argyle doggy sweater over her head. "You look awfully fixed up to be going out with only Isabelle. Is this what you and Lila were doing all day?"

I shrug. I must have been delusional to think my mom wouldn't notice my makeover.

"You look very pretty," she says. "Very grown-up."

"Thanks."

Mom chews her lip. "Is something going on?"

"*No*, nothing's going on. I'm going to a movie with Isabelle. There *might* be a guy there she knows. So I put on makeup and curled my hair. That's all."

Mom smiles broadly. She actually looks happy that I've been withholding information from her. "Well, now. That makes more sense."

I roll my eyes.

"Don't worry," she continues, "I'm not going to embarrass you. Am I, Camille?" Camille doesn't reply. She probably knows the answer's yes. Mom holds Camille up high so she can examine me too. "Doesn't your sister look pretty?"

Camille and I lock eyes. For once, she doesn't say anything.

"Okay, Mom—enough doggy talk. Isabelle's waiting."

— — — —

We pick up Isabelle and head to the big movie theater attached to the mall. Aside from driving with a fully clothed dog in her lap, my mom manages not to say or do anything horrible the entire ride. She doesn't even try to pump Isabelle for information.

Isabelle and I get out of the car a block before the theater. It's our first chance to talk without my mom hearing us, and I suddenly feel shy. I'm out with one of the coolest girls at Eastley, crashing her date, secretly hoping to *steal* her date, and I don't have any idea what I'm doing.

"You look really nice," she says to me. She's carrying her

coat so her outfit shows, even though we have to walk a bit. "I like your hair."

"Thanks." Feeling stupid, I take off my coat too, since it appears to be proper date etiquette to be out in the freezing cold with just our makeup and flirty sweaters to keep us warm.

Isabelle's wearing a tight-fitting pale yellow turtleneck, a short plaid skirt, and tights with a pair of brown riding boots. She looks like prep-school girl meets *Vogue*. I thank my lucky stars I had Lila dress me, or I'd be completely invisible next to her.

Isabelle flips her hair over her shoulder and points. "That way. We're meeting the guys by the ticket window."

"The guys? Plural?"

"Yeah." Isabelle smiles at me, all wide-eyed innocence. "Epp and I thought it might be fun to double, so he asked a friend to come along. Is that okay?"

My mouth drops into an O shape and freezes. Isabelle got me a date. I have a date. I'm no longer tagging along on *her* date; now I have my own to worry about. "S-sure," I stammer. "What's his name?"

"Oh, I'm not sure who he brought. But all of his friends are awesome. We'll have fun." She walks quickly toward the ticket window and I follow, trying to calm myself. I don't know why I'm so thrown, but I guess I thought when I'd have my very first date ever, I'd know about it ahead of time.

In front of the theater two guys stand with their backs to us. One is definitely Epp, with thick dark hair and some nicely fitted jeans. The other, I assume, is my date. He's a little shorter, and he's wearing jeans also, with a heavy flannel shirt that looks like it might be a jacket. He has dirty blond hair that's so curly it looks like it can't be brushed.

This is it. This is my first date.

I clear my throat so my voice will behave, and as I do, Isabelle goes up to Epp and puts her hands on his hips.

He turns around and smiles, then kisses her. The kiss lasts at least ten seconds, which is *very long* when you're watching. When he finally pulls away, he puts his arm around her and gives me a friendly smile. It's not his high-voltage smile, but maybe he can't show me that one when Isabelle's around.

"Taryn, hey. This is Pete." Epp gestures at the curly-headed guy, who looks me over.

Pete's cute, and he has nice teeth, but next to Epp he's just an ordinary guy. He doesn't have the sparkle. "Hey," he says.

"Hey," I say back. I try to remind myself that having Pete around will make the evening easier, but inside I'm annoyed there's one more person for Epp to talk to other than me. And if Epp likes me, even just a little bit, why would he want me to meet another guy?

"Pete plays soccer at St. Ivan's," Isabelle says, looking pleased with Epp's choice of escort for me. "Taryn's a great writer," she tells him. "She's on our school paper and she's doing an article about student athletes."

Isabelle has a talent of saying whatever she wants and making it seem true just by saying it. She has no idea whether or not I'm a good writer. But for some reason, when she says it, I feel like I am.

Pete and I smile uneasily at each other, but neither of us says anything.

"We should get tickets," Epp says, saving us.

He and Isabelle hold hands and walk up to the window. Pete and I follow. I wonder which of us feels more awkward. He doesn't look terribly excited about being fixed up with me, but maybe he's just shy. If he's Epp's friend, he's probably a nice guy.

When in doubt, talk about the weather. "It's cold out," I say.

"Put your jacket on," he replies. He doesn't say it rudely, but in a way that makes me feel ridiculous for standing outside in just my sweater.

So I pull my jacket on and try to act nonchalant. Epp and Isabelle stand in front of us in line, talking, completely oblivious to what's going on behind them. I hear Epp tell Isabelle she looks beautiful, and I melt a little just hearing him say the words.

Pete stands silently next to me. "So, have you heard anything about this movie?" I ask.

"Yeah, it looks stupid," he says. "Why would someone kill their own twin?"

"Jealousy? Maybe the twin's better looking."

He shakes his head. "Nah. That's *really* stupid."

Why did he come, if it wasn't to be on a date or to see the movie? I decide to keep quiet. Maybe you aren't supposed to talk on a blind date—just stand around like idiots.

After a few minutes of silently inching forward in line, it's Epp's turn. He pays for tickets for himself and Isabelle, and Pete steps up to the window.

I panic, realizing I have no idea who should pay. Since we're on a date, is he supposed to pay? Epp and Isabelle invited me out with them first, without a date, but then brought him for me. Does that mean that I pay? Especially since I'm using them for the article? Or do we pay separately, but only after both offering to pay?

I pretend to fiddle with the zipper on my jacket and let him stay ahead of me in line.

"Two for *Twin Killer*," he says into the window.

I pull some money out of my pocket and show it to him. "Here," I say. "Thanks."

He looks down at it, surprised. "Don't worry about it." Then he hands me a ticket, opens the door for me, and we walk inside.

"Popcorn?" Epp asks us. Isabelle and I shake our heads, probably both imagining kernels in our teeth. Pete shrugs. "Well, I'm going to get some," Epp says, and walks over to the food counter.

Isabelle, Pete, and I stand uncertainly for a minute. Then Isabelle speaks. "So, what's new, Pete?"

"Absolutely nothing."

"You should talk to Taryn about soccer—I'm sure she'd love to put you in the article, too."

Pete checks out the movie posters behind her head. "No thanks, I don't do interviews."

Isabelle gives him a really funny look, like he's her kid and she's asked him to take out the trash but he won't. A look like, *Why won't you just behave?* Then she looks at me and rolls her eyes. This makes me feel better, because now I know it's not just me.

I decide to seize the opportunity to be alone with Epp, even for just a second. "I'm going to help with the popcorn." I walk toward the counter, removing my coat again so my sweater shows. I'm very aware of how big my chest looks in Mary's bra. It's kind of embarrassing. I miss my smaller, less obvious boobs.

I stand self-consciously next to Epp. "Need any help?"

He has a giant slurpee, popcorn, and nachos on the counter. "Sure," he says. Now that we're alone, his high-voltage smile has returned. I feel myself swoon a bit. "Grab the nachos."

"Okay." I wrack my brain, trying to think of something interesting to say. "It's really crowded here tonight."

"Yeah, it's always like this on Saturdays. Even when bad movies are playing."

"Thanks for inviting Pete," I say. "You didn't have to. I hope you didn't drag him along or anything."

Epp gives me a sheepish look, like I caught him copying out of a library book. Apparently there was some dragging. No wonder Pete's so grumpy. "He's hard to get to know. But he's a good guy. And you're a pretty girl—how could he not like you?"

I force myself to keep walking calmly, as if nothing happened. But something did happen—*Epp told me I'm pretty.* I

want to say thank you, say something, but we're already at
Pete and Isabelle.

"We'd better grab seats," Epp says. "It's packed."

Isabelle grabs Epp's arm and they lead us into the theater.
The place is jammed, and the only four seats together are in
the first few rows.

I start to move toward them as Isabelle says, "I guess we
should split up."

Pete and I both look at her, alarmed. Split up? We don't
even *know* each other.

"We could all sit in front," Epp says nicely.

I picture myself sitting next to him, his arm brushing mine
during the movie. I smile unconsciously.

"I'll get a headache up front," Isabelle tells us. "Sorry,
guys. We'll see you after?" She smiles at me apologetically
and leads Epp toward the back of the theater. I watch him
walk away and feel myself deflate.

Pete and I shuffle our feet, neither of us wanting to take
charge. Finally his man-sense kicks in and he realizes that
he's the guy.

"Where do you want to sit?" he asks, with all the excitement of getting a flu shot.

"The middle is fine." I'm not going to let Pete's attitude
bother me. This is my first date, and I'm going to try and
enjoy it. I realize I still have Epp's nachos, which is a good
thing, since I was too nervous to eat dinner.

Pete pushes his way through to some seats in the middle
of a row. We're definitely squished in, but at least we can see

the screen. We both avoid the armrest between us and try to sit as upright as possible. I check out the other people sitting around us. It's mostly people our age, either in groups or on dates. I realize that people checking me out will notice that I'm on a date. With Pete. Who, even though he's not Epp, is still a good-looking guy.

"Nacho?" I offer.

He shakes his head. "What do you call cheese that isn't yours?" he asks.

I look at him oddly. "Huh?"

"Nacho cheese." He rolls his head back and laughs at his joke. Then he slips his flannel shirt/jacket off and flops it over the back of his chair. He's wearing a short-sleeved T-shirt underneath, and for some reason I'm embarrassed seeing his bare arms. Like he's getting naked or something, when really he only took off his jacket.

"So, you and Isabelle are good friends?" he asks. "I'm surprised I haven't met you before."

"Not really. I just came tonight to ask them both questions for my article."

"Oh." He looks thoughtful.

I wonder if I said something wrong. Maybe Isabelle told him she and I are good friends? "You hang out with them a lot?"

"With Epp, yeah. I thought he and I were going to shoot pool tonight. Then he called me and asked if I minded if Isabelle came, and if we went to the movies instead of pool." He reaches over for a handful of nachos, dunks them in cheese, and jams them in his mouth.

So that's how they got him here. I guess neither of us knew we were being set up. "I didn't know you were coming either," I admit. "I thought I was tagging along on Isabelle's date."

"I'm glad I came though," he says, smiling at me. "These nachos are great."

I don't answer, unsure if he meant he's glad he came because of the nachos or because he met me.

The movie begins and I try to concentrate. Unfortunately, it's a pretty awful movie. The story jumps around and there are a lot of those moments where the music gets really scary and even though you know something is about to jump out at you, you still freak out when it does.

I don't want to scream in front of Pete so I detach myself from the action on the screen and just nibble at my nachos and think. I picture Epp and Isabelle cuddled up somewhere making out, which is what people should do during a movie this bad.

Beside me, Pete shifts in his seat and rubs his hands against his jeans. I'd almost forgotten he was there. He seems to be paying attention to the movie. I want to get up and go to the bathroom, but the thought of climbing over ten people to get to the aisle stops me. Instead I sit with my knees pressed tight together and try to think of nice things. Christmas presents. Good grades on my exams. Being able to drive soon. As I'm picturing myself handing in an exceptionally well-written article for the *Mighty Quill*, Pete leans over and plants one on me.

I'm so shocked I just sit there, my mouth immobile. He's

not kissing me in the slobbery, tongue-weapon kind of way you get warned about; it's more like the tasteful kisses you see on family TV shows. After a long minute, he pulls away and sits back in his seat, like he's paying attention to the movie again.

My mind is racing and my lips feel funny, sort of smooshed and tingly. I don't know if this is officially a date now, or if it means that Pete likes me or what. Or maybe it's just required that if you go to a movie together, you make out. All I know is that I've finally had my first kiss, and I don't even know the guy. I feel excited, but at the same time, let down.

Pete sits quietly through the rest of the movie and finishes the nachos. He doesn't say or do anything to indicate something unusual happened between us. Of course, it probably wasn't his first kiss, so it probably wasn't unusual to him.

When the lights come up, I avoid making eye contact with him. I'm not sure how I should act. We shuffle down the row to the aisle and walk single file out into the lobby to wait for Isabelle and Epp, almost like we aren't even together.

As soon as we see them, Isabelle gives me a questioning look and Epp grins at us. "Nice lipstick," he says to Pete.

I look directly at Pete for the first time and see a smear of mauve lip-gloss on the corner of his mouth.

"Whoops," he says, not sounding the least bit sorry. In fact, he winks at me, which throws me even more, because he doesn't seem at all like the winking type. I give my own mouth a quick swipe with the back of my wrist, feeling like I've just been caught doing something really bad.

Thankfully, Isabelle saves me by changing the subject. "Let's go somewhere we can talk about Taryn's article."

The guys say they're hungry, so we leave the theater through the mall exit and find a table at Taco Burger. They go to the counter to get us each an order of chicken tacos.

"Looks like you and Pete hit it off," Isabelle says. She sounds pleased, and kind of proud, as if she set us up when really Epp was the one who brought him.

"I don't really know him," I say hastily. I want to explain that he just leaned over and kissed me, completely out the blue. "It was . . . unexpected."

She looks at me knowingly, like she gets what I'm saying without me saying it. "He's a nice guy—you should go out with him. You'd be a great couple."

Hearing the word "couple" surprises me a little. I would really, really like to be a great couple—with Epp. But I'm flattered Isabelle would want me dating one of Epp's good friends. It means we'd probably be out together all the time.

"You think so?" I ask.

She nods. "Definitely. You're perfect together."

I want to ask her why but the guys return with trays. Isabelle and I pick at our tacos while Pete and Epp wolf theirs down like they haven't eaten for weeks.

I remember that I'm supposed to be talking about my article, so I ask Pete and Epp about Isabelle's theory about sports at single-sex schools versus co-ed. Since they're guys, they don't really get it.

"Why wouldn't girls' sports get attention at a co-ed school?" Pete asks. He takes a long sip of his soda and barely stifles a burp.

"Because usually the boys' teams get more support," Isabelle says, ignoring his lack of manners. "And the females cheer for them. Have you ever seen a male cheerleading squad for the girls?"

"There are guy cheerleaders," Epp replies. He has taco sauce on his lip but it actually looks cute. I catch myself staring for a second and look away.

"Yes, but usually in college or on the *one* cheerleading team schools have that mostly supports the male teams," Isabelle argues. "That's why Taryn and I go to a girls' school—everything is all about the girls. Our class officers, our sports teams, everything."

"You use guys in your school musicals," says Pete. "If you're so anti-guy, you should do the male parts in drag." He and Epp both laugh loudly.

Isabelle and I exchange a look. "We're not anti-guy," I explain patiently. "And we're not saying which option is the best. We're just discussing what the differences are. That's the point of the article." For a minute I forget I invented the article and was forced onto the newspaper. I've started to get into my topic and really think about it.

"Okay, you win." Epp wipes his mouth with a napkin. "When's it due?"

"The rough draft's due Monday."

"That sucks," Pete and Epp say at the same time.

"We have that huge French translation due this week, too," says Isabelle. "Are you going to have to do all that tomorrow?"

I nod and everyone looks at me sympathetically. Sitting together under the bright lights of Taco Burger, talking about my article, I feel like part of a group. Even though I didn't know or talk to these people a few weeks ago, it seems like we're on our way to being friends.

Chapter Ten

Sunday morning I wake up with a headache. It's going to be a long day. Not only do I have to call Lila and relay the dirty details from last night, but I have to do all of my homework, start my French translation, and write a rough draft for Carla.

I decide to call Lila first. "Helllloooo?" she answers.

"Stop answering the phone like that!" I snap.

"Like what?"

"Like you're an obscene phone caller."

Lila sighs. "I'm guessing it didn't go well."

"Actually, it did. We kissed."

"*You kissed Epp?*"

"No," I reply. "That's the problem. I kissed *Pete.*"

I'm pretty sure I hear Lila's brains rattle over the phone. "I don't understand," she says. "Who's Pete, and why'd you kiss him?"

"He's a friend of Epp's from St. Ivan's. Isabelle asked Epp to invite him so we could double-date."

"Oh she did, did she?"

"*Lila.* Don't say it like that. She did it to be nice, so I wouldn't feel like I was tagging along on her date with Epp."

"Mmm-hmm. Sure she did. She probably figured out you're after her man, so she threw a guy at you to get you to stop."

I don't buy it. "She and I are friendly now, Lila, whether you believe it or not."

She mmm-hmms into the phone again. "So what's this Pete guy like?"

"He's . . . cute. He's got curly hair and nice teeth, but he's a little hard to talk to. He has a car, though, and he drove us all home."

"Oh?" Now Lila sounds interested. "When'd you kiss him? What was it like?"

I can tell Lila is envious about my kiss but trying not to show it. In one night we've gone from being even-steven to me dating, kissing, and being driven home by a guy. "It just happened, during the movie. And it was . . . nice." I close my eyes and press my lips together, trying to remember how it felt.

"Nice? Is that all you can say?"

I'm a little uncomfortable discussing this part. The kiss, even though it probably didn't mean anything, is private. I don't want to explain that Pete and I hardly talked beforehand and it came out of the clear blue and I didn't know what to do and I have no idea if I'll ever hear from him again. "Yes, nice," I say insistently.

"C'mon, Taryn. You know that if I got kissed, I'd tell you

every detail. How did it happen? And how long did it last? Was there tongue?"

"It's personal, Lila! Geez."

Lila is silent on the other end of the phone. "Fine," she says finally. "Then tell me what happened with Epp and Isabelle. Did you get to be alone with him at all?"

"Yeah, for a second. But then they sat together at the movies, not with us." I pause, remembering the sight of Epp and Isabelle kissing, holding hands, snuggling in the backseat of Pete's car. Seeing them out on a date made it pretty clear that they are Together. "They seemed really happy."

"Happy?"

"Yeah." I sigh to myself so she won't hear me.

"So what does that mean?" Lila asks. "Are you giving up?"

"I gave up before, when I decided to focus on the article. But now I really mean it, I guess."

Lila is quiet for a second. "I still think he likes you, Taryn."

Deep down, part of me agrees. I know he liked me when we were alone. "Let's talk about something else. I'm going to put together my draft for the article today. I have to show it to Carla tomorrow."

"That stinks," Lila says, playing along. "But at least you can put the *Quill* on your college applications."

"Have you been talking to my mother?"

Lila ignores the question. "How'd the bra work out?"

Bra or no bra, I can't compete with Isabelle. But I did end up with a surprise date last night, a compliment from Epp, and a kiss from Pete. "You know, it was kind of lucky for me. Can I keep it awhile?"

"Sure—until Christmas break, I guess. Then Mary'll be home, and she might notice."

"That's only two weeks."

"It's not like it'll help with exams." Lila laughs. "Go work on your article. I'm going to watch a movie."

"Thanks for rubbing it in. See you tomorrow."

"No problem. Later, alligator."

— — — —

Lugging my backpack, I settle at the dining-room table, the only place in the house I can really spread out. I locate the notes from my interviews with Isabelle and Epp and pull out two articles I found online about high school sports and reread them.

I can't believe this is all I have.

I sit and stare at my notes. Mostly they're observations about Epp or Isabelle with a few sports-related questions thrown in. I can't write an entire article about a popular sophomore couple who both play sports. That's not an article—it's me obsessing.

After an hour of staring blankly at my notebook, I don't even have a first sentence. I want to write something so good that Carla will think I'm brilliant, Isabelle will think I'm cool, and Epp will want me to go out with him. But there's no way I can write something that will do all of that.

I decide to give up and summarize everything and show it to Carla. I'll tell her I'm having trouble and need some help getting started. After all, I've never done this before, and she is the editor. I write a quick paragraph about Isabelle's theory and then begin my homework. Mom and Camille come in while I'm doing Trig.

"May we join you for lunch?" Mom asks. She's balancing three plates: two with sandwiches, chips, and pickles, and one with boiled beef and spaghetti noodles.

"Sure, c'mon in."

Mom places the sandwiches in front of my chair and hers, then pulls a dishtowel from her back pocket, lays it on the floor, and puts the boiled-beef plate on top of it. Camille races over and inspects her lunch. Satisfied, she begins chowing down.

"You look busy," Mom says. "How's your article coming along?"

"It's all right," I reply, my mouth full. My turkey and Swiss is delicious. My mom sure does make a good sandwich.

"Can I help?"

"I don't know."

"Can I *try*?"

"I guess." I push the summary I wrote at her and take a bite of my pickle. It's the smelly kind that makes your fingers and breath reek for a day or two but is worth it.

Mom skims my summary. She puts it down and eats her pickle. Then she picks it back up and skims again.

"What exactly is the article supposed to be about?" she asks.

"Originally it was about the difference between guys' and girls' sports, but now I want it to be about why playing sports at a co-ed school would be different than at a single-sex school. And I have a male perspective and a female perspective."

"And you chose *Isabelle* as your female athlete?"

"*Yeeeesssss,*" I say defensively. "She plays tennis."

"But aren't there girls at your school who are more serious than Isabelle? Girls who play three sports? Girls on varsity? Girls with athletic scholarships to college?"

"It's a high school paper, Mom." You'd think she was the editor of the *Baltimore Sun*. "And Isabelle's really smart. The new hypothesis was her idea."

"That may be, but if you're going to do something, you need to do it well. And you are not doing this well. This looks half-hearted, Taryn." Mom's voice has that sharp, disappointed tone, which makes me angry and miserable at the same time.

"Why did you pick these two people?" she goes on. "The boy looks okay—he plays two sports—but he's also only a sophomore."

"I chose Isabelle because we're friends," I explain, "and the guy is Isabelle's boyfriend. I asked her if she knew anyone I could interview and she suggested him."

"Well, it's not very strategic. You need to talk to a coach. And some more serious athletes. Why did you pick this topic when you don't even *like* sports?" Mom's voice is grating and I'm afraid if she keeps nagging at me, I'll flip out.

"Okay, okay," I say quickly. "I'll talk to the editor tomorrow. I know it needs a lot of work."

"How are your grades?"

"Fiiiiine." I try to keep my voice steady. I know a lecture

about Christmas and my exams is next and I don't want to get into it. I still haven't answered my dad's email and I don't want to. As soon as I tell him I'm coming, I'll have to tell Mom, and then she'll look at me with hurt eyes for the next two weeks. "I'm going to fix the article, Mom, really."

Mom picks Camille off the floor and cuddles her against her chest. She looks like a fuzzy white muff warming Mom's hands. They both look at me worriedly. Well, Mom looks at me worriedly. Camille looks bored—probably because we're talking about me.

"Have you bitten off more than you can chew?" Mom asks.

I open my mouth to show her it's empty, but she doesn't laugh. "Don't worry about me so much, Mom."

"I have to worry about you. I'm your mother."

I bite my tongue before telling her the person she should be worrying about is herself. But I've got too much homework to start a fight, so I keep my mouth shut and go back to my Trig problems.

— — — —

I look for Carla at school so I can talk to her alone before the *Quill's* meeting. I need to ask for help and I don't want to do it in front of the other Quillions. But she isn't in the office the two times I run up there, and I don't see her in the lounge or the cafeteria, so I'm stuck worrying about the meeting all day.

When I walk into French class last period, Isabelle motions for me to sit next to her. I almost look around to make sure she means me.

"Hey," she says, as I slide into the seat. "How was the rest of your weekend?"

"It was good." I pull out my books and act natural, like I always sit here and talk to her before class. "Thanks for setting up Saturday night, by the way. I had a great time."

She smiles and looks relieved. "I'm glad—I was afraid you might be mad we brought Pete without telling you."

"No, not at all. Maybe we can do it again sometime."

Isabelle smiles even bigger. "Yeah, we should! We go to the movies a lot. Or bowling. I'll say something to Epp about it."

It's just normal conversation, but after our double date I wonder if I now rank as one of Isabelle's friends, one that she goes out with on weekends. Even though I know how Lila would feel about that, I like the idea. "Sure, I'd love to."

"Epp thinks you're great," she says, digging in her backpack for a pen. "He likes you more than a lot of my other friends."

I open and close my mouth but nothing comes out. There are so many ways to interpret that comment that I don't know how to respond.

Isabelle keeps talking like nothing remarkable was said. "Did you do the translation assignment yet?" she asks.

I open my book and force myself to focus. "I started it yesterday, but I was working on the article, so I didn't get very far."

"I finished mine, if you want to borrow it."

I try not to look stunned. Isabelle Graham is offering to let me copy her homework? Something that probably took hours to do? Not only is that very un-Eastley, it's something only a really, really good friend would offer. "Th-thanks. That would be great."

She fishes a paper out of her binder and hands it to me. I slip it into my notebook, amazed this is the same person I thought was a total snob a few weeks ago.

Madame comes in to start class and everyone stops talking. Isabelle turns around to face the board and I stare at the back of her head, wondering.

— — — —

I head up to the newspaper meeting after class feeling very uneasy. Like last week, the Quillions are sitting along both sides of the carpeted hall, their legs a big jumble in the middle. I'm right on time but I'm the last one to arrive.

I sit down hurriedly and pull out a notebook.

"Taryn!" Carla calls from the far end. "You're here. Why don't you give us an update on your article?"

Fourteen of the school's biggest brains look at me expectantly as I collect myself enough to speak. I'd planned on talking to Carla alone. This is worse than giving a class presentation. In Latin. With food in my teeth.

"Actually, I wanted to talk to you about that," I begin uncertainly. "I'm having some problems pulling it all together—"

"That's normal," Carla interrupts. "It's your first piece. Read us what you have, and maybe we can help."

I take a deep breath. Everyone is staring at me expectantly, waiting to hear my brilliance. "I haven't started writing yet. I have, um, notes. I wanted to go over them with you first, before I . . . " I finish by making a lot of useless hand gestures.

Carla nods and adjusts her glasses. "Gotcha," she says. "We'll talk for a few minutes after, okay?"

The meeting goes on and other girls read snippets from their articles. One is writing about the Russian teacher going on sabbatical for a year to Moscow. Another wrote about a seventh grader who was named a Junior National Fencing champion. I had no idea people really fenced, especially twelve-year-olds. The articles all sound interesting, fully researched, and well written.

After the meeting, feeling like a complete, moronic failure compared to the other Quillions, I follow Carla into the office. She sits down at the messiest desk, pulls open the bottom drawer, and retrieves a diet soda. I wonder if she's the one who drank all three hundred or so empty cans behind her.

"This office is always cold," she explains, popping the top. "So sodas stay nice and chilled in the desk. Now, what's the problem?"

I debate what to tell her. I want her to think I've put a lot of effort into the article, but I also know it'll be hard to fool her.

"Well," I say, "the article's not working. I did two interviews, and worked on my hypothesis, but I don't think the idea's as interesting as I thought it would be."

"I see." Carla frowns and pushes up her glasses. I wonder if she has a button on her desk that will make the floor open up beneath me and suck me down to the boiler room. "Well,

Taryn, the good news is, this happens to every reporter. Stories and ideas change; they take on a life of their own. Sometimes you don't write the story, the story writes *you.*"

I want to ask her what that's supposed to mean, but I keep quiet.

"The bad news is, you have to work through it, because I've already told Mrs. Hert, the *Quill's* advisor, about your story, and she wants it to run. So I need your final draft next week."

I gulp and suddenly I can hardly breathe. What is happening to me? I'm pretending to be a reporter, which, after hearing those other girls talk about their stories, I'm clearly *not,* and digging myself into a huge hole of lies because of a guy who's not even a possibility. And whose girlfriend is setting me up with guys, taking me out with her, and letting me borrow her French homework.

"Carla, I can't write this article," I blurt out. Her eyebrows pop up from behind her glasses, and I can see she wants to question me, but I just keep talking. "It started out as a lie, because I met this awesome guy and I wanted to do the article to get to know him better. But it turns out he has a girlfriend, and she's really nice, so it's horrible for me to like her boyfriend. I'm so sorry, because I know I've wasted your time. But *I can't do the article.*"

I press my lips together and hold my breath. Even though Carla's not a teacher, I wonder if there isn't some disciplinary action she can take against me, like a demerit, or taking two points off of my GPA for lying. This is Eastley, after all, and I'm sure I've just broken some tenet of our honor code.

"Wow." Carla stares at me in wonder for a moment. Then she takes a big sip of her soda. "If that isn't a good story, I don't know what is."

My eyes widen. "Are you serious?"

She nods. "Absolutely. Do you want to write about that instead?"

"No!" I reply. "I don't want to write anything! I don't even want to be on the stupid paper. I want to forget this whole thing ever happened and not embarrass myself any further."

Carla looks taken aback and slightly offended. I probably shouldn't have said "stupid paper."

"Okay," she says slowly, "if that's what you want. We'll kill the article, and you're off the paper."

"Really?"

"Sure. This happens all the time." She clears her throat. "Well, not this *exactly,* but sometimes things don't work out. I'll have to ask for your *Quill* pen back, though."

I automatically reach into my backpack and she starts laughing. "I'm kidding, relax. Who's the girlfriend, anyway? Does she go to Eastley?"

For some reason, I tell her. "Yeah—Isabelle Graham."

"She's on the tennis team, right? With the long red hair?" I nod. She whistles through her teeth. "Good luck with that."

"What do you mean?" I ask. "Good luck with what? I'm not *doing* anything."

"I know," she says, sounding amused. "I just meant, good

luck with things. Fare thee well. And if you ever decide you want to make it up to me by helping with editing or layout, you know where to find me."

I nod violently. "Yes, I do. Thanks, Carla. Really."

"No problem. Merry Christmas."

Lila and I lounge in her room after school, drinking orange soda and listening to her sister's CDs. I've been so consumed with dog walking, interviewing, and lying that it's been weeks since I've been to her house.

Lila sits at her desk, checking email. "So the article's dead," she says.

"Yep—dead as a doornail. Dead as a deadline. I'm done with the article and I'm done with liking someone unattainable," I announce. "I'm going to channel that energy into getting an A on my Latin exam."

"That's a noble goal. And only *slightly* less unattainable."

"Thank you." I grab the remote and skip ahead on the CD to get to a song I like. "I'm going to see my dad for a few days after Christmas," I tell her. "But maybe we can start studying for Latin together when I get back."

"But you went up there for Thanksgiving," Lila says.

"I know, but we have two weeks off, and I'll stay with my mom for Christmas Day and everything. And dad's house is more fun for Christmas because my uncles and grandparents are around, and they really celebrate. You know my mom is sort of a Scrooge."

"Are you definitely going?"

"I think so. I need a break, you know?" I don't mention that even though I'm pretty sure I've made my decision, I've been too chicken to tell either of my parents. "Can I check my email when you're done?"

"Yeah, one sec—I'm emailing Mary. Can I tell her you wore her bra for your very first hot hookup?"

"*No.* Do *not* tell her that."

"She'd probably be honored." Lila finishes typing and moves over to the bed. "It's all yours."

I plop down onto her chair, log on to my email, and there, between an overdue notice from the school library and a FREE OFFER for PRESCRIPTION DRUGS, is an email from HARGESTY, PETE.

"Oh my God!" My fingers freeze. I can't click on it.

"What? What?"

"There's an email from Pete! I can't open it. I'm too scared."

Lila peers over my shoulder and looks at the screen. "No subject line. Hmm."

"What does that mean? No subject line?"

"It means no subject line," Lila says. "Open it."

"No!"

"You have to. What if he really likes you and he's asking you out again?"

I shake my head. "No way. I probably left something in his car. Or he wants to recommend I go to kissing school."

"Oh, for Pete's sake." She laughs. "Ooh, I made a pun. Get it?"

"Lila!"

She laughs again. "It was punny."

"It *wasn't*."

"Open it now or I will."

"Okay, but go sit on the bed so I can read it in private." Lila grouches but moves back to the bed. I click on the email. My stomach feels like it's full of bad seafood.

> You busy after school tomorrow? I can pick you up at Eastley
> at 3:30.
>
> Pete

I read the email thirty times but I can't figure out exactly what Pete is asking me. "Lila, c'mere. I need you to translate."

She hops up and stands behind me again. "'You busy after school tomorrow?'" she reads. "'I can pick you up at Eastley at three thirty. Pete.'"

I glare at her. "I said I need you to *translate*. Not *read aloud*."

"I was trying to get the tone."

"Is this a date?" I ask. "Or does he want to talk about my article? Or does he need someone to help him pick out a tie?"

Lila shrugs her shoulders. "It could mean any of those things. You have to give him credit—he's good at being mysterious."

"Someone would have to work hard to be this vague. Am I right?"

"Very right," Lila agrees. "Are you going to go?"

I can't tell from her tone whether she thinks I should go or shouldn't. "I don't know. We hardly talked the other night, and this would be the two of us alone together. I don't even *know* him."

"You knew him well enough to kiss him," she reminds me. Her voice has more than a hint of green in it.

"Yeah, well, that just happened. It's hard to explain."

Lila lounges back on her bed and flips open her magazine again. "The way I see it, a guy is a guy and a date is a date. Go and see what happens. Maybe you'll end up liking him and he'll have a cute friend for me."

"He does have a cute friend—Epp, remember? Who I have vowed not to like anymore because he's Isabelle's. But I do want to go. For curiosity's sake, at least." I sigh and stare at Pete's email. "When did my life become so complicated? What about my A in Latin?"

"You can study when you're dead, Taryn. Dead as a door-nail."

— — — —

At three thirty the next day, in freshly applied makeup and my most flattering school jumper, I walk out to the carpool pick-up circle.

I look pretty good. My hair is slightly wavy from curling it this morning, and I only have two tiny zits high up on my forehead. The giant chin zit cleared up as soon as I quit the article. Even though it's cold, I'm carrying my coat instead of wearing it. I learned something from my first date.

Cars packed with girls in blue uniforms are coming and going and I search for Pete's sedan. I emailed him back at Lila's, *Okay, see you at 3:30*, trying to be as cryptic as he was. He didn't reply. I wanted to write, *Is this a date?* or *What's this about?* but Lila convinced me it was better to play it cool.

So here I am, cooling my heels.

3:40.

3:45.

Several carpool moms frown at me for not wearing my coat, and I'm about to put it on when Pete's car pulls up. I walk over slowly, feeling a lot like I do before I go to the dentist.

I open the door and climb in. "Hi," I say casually. *Let him do all the talking,* Lila told me. *Be quiet and let him tell you what's going on.*

Pete's wearing his blazer and khakis. He's loosened his tie, and I catch a whiff of spearmint gum coming from him.

"Hey," he says. "You hungry?"

"Sure." Actually, I'm not. I'm too nervous to be hungry. But food definitely constitutes a date. I think.

"Want to go to Blue Street Diner?"

I nod. "Sure," I say again.

Pete doesn't talk as he drives. It's very hard not to ask why he emailed me, so I force myself to look out the window and count red cars.

"So," he says, finally.

Fourteen red cars. "So," I reply.

Silence again. Sixteen red cars. Pete's car is a manual, and he seems to like shifting gears, because he does it a lot. He drives with both feet like he's playing hopscotch. Every time he pushes in the clutch, I catch a glimpse of his bare ankle. Apparently Pete doesn't wear socks. I wonder what his shoes smell like.

We pull into the parking lot and my stomach flutters, but it's an excited flutter now, not a nervous one. Blue Street Diner is a cool place to hang out. It's not like Sam's, which is *the* place to hang out; it's a more low-key version. I've never been there except with Lila. Now I'm walking in with a guy from St. Ivan's.

Pete opens his door and hops out. He takes off his jacket, pulls his loosened tie over his head, and starts unbuttoning his shirt. I squint at him. What is he doing? It's December.

He strips down to a gray T-shirt that says *Towson Summer Soccer League* in crackly black letters. He's now wearing just the T-shirt, khakis, and shoes with no socks. He tosses his clothes into the backseat, pats his pockets, and locks the car.

I follow him toward the diner, worried now it's not cool to be seen in your school clothes at the diner.

He holds the door open for me, and a hostess seats us at a booth in the corner. There's a mini jukebox on the table, with an overwhelming choice of eleven songs. I sneak a peek at the other tables and don't see a single person in a school uniform. Oh well.

Pete opens his menu and studies it, really studies it, like it's a list of vocabulary words for the SATs.

"You hungry?" he asks me for the second time.

Good grief. "Yes," I lie again.

He cracks a smile and rubs his eyes. He rubs them aggressively, like he's wiping away his eyeballs. When he pulls his hands away, his cheeks are red and his eyes are watery. His eye color is somewhere between dark gray and dark blue. Not a color you could think of a good name for.

A red-lipsticked waitress appears and takes our order. Pete gets a soda, a milkshake, and a cheeseburger with fries. I order the Cobb salad and a ginger ale. I don't want anything with condiments or that I have to eat with my hands, which limits me to about two items on the menu.

The waitress brings our sodas and Pete's milkshake. He offers me a sip but I shake my head, no. It feels too soon to share a milkshake.

"So," he says for probably the fifth time. "That was fun the other night."

I sip my ginger ale and think about my answer. "Uh-huh," I say.

"You wanna go out with me?"

I freeze. My immediate instinct is to say, *Are you serious?* but I keep my mouth closed and my face blank. This doesn't make sense. He can't be asking what I think he's asking. "Do you mean, *go out*, go out?" I ask, looking at his plate instead of his face.

"I mean, goooo ouuuut tooogether." He says each word slowly so my socially ignorant brain will understand.

I sip some ginger ale and swish it around my mouth, trying

to look too busy to answer. The food arrives, and he calmly grabs the ketchup, coats his burger, and takes a big bite.

"It's no big deal," he says, his mouth full. "But there's a party Saturday, and Epp and Isabelle are going, and I thought we could go."

I'm an idiot. I thought he was asking me to go out with him, like, be his girlfriend, but he was only asking to go out on Saturday. And Epp and Isabelle will be there, so I can hang out with them, too.

Pete's already halfway through his cheeseburger. I look right into his bluish, grayish eyes and say, "Sure, sounds like fun."

He takes a slurp of milkshake. "Cool."

I pick at the avocado in my Cobb salad, feeling surprisingly spectacular. I wasn't sure how this meeting with Pete would turn out, but now I have a date to a party Saturday.

"So, um, have you and Epp been friends a long time?" I ask him. Even though I'm no longer allowing myself to like Epp, there's no harm in asking about him.

"Yeah. We've gone to school together since first grade or something. Same with you and Isabelle?"

"We've known each other since first grade, too," I say honestly.

"She's a great girl," he says. "Seriously pretty."

I take a bite of my salad and don't answer. I'm sure Pete didn't mean that the way it sounded. After all, he likes me enough to want to go out with me.

He leans back in the booth and I study him. He's not Epp, but he does have nice shoulders—they're broad, but not big.

His arms still have a little summer tan on them. If we're going out again, we might as well get to know each other.

I point at his T-shirt. "So, you play soccer year-round?"

"Yep—indoor and outdoor." He's got ketchup and mustard on his face but continues to eat his fries without wiping it off. "You play any sports?" he asks me.

"No, I'm not very coordinated. I'm better at watching."

"I guess you're more scholarly," he jokes. At least, I hope he's joking. It's not very flattering to be referred to as "scholarly." "How'd the article turn out?"

"The article? It, uh, didn't work out. The editor cut it last minute from the issue, because it was full." I glance up to see if he believes me.

"That stinks. I'm sure you worked hard on it."

I don't want to get stuck talking about the article, in case I put my foot in my mouth, so I change the subject back to his soccer team and let him talk.

When I've picked all the good stuff out of my salad, Pete wipes his face clean and crumples his napkin. "Let's get out of here." He signals the waitress and she brings over the check.

I put my wallet out of my backpack, but he waves it away and pays the bill. I think that makes this my second official date. And I have a third one on Saturday.

All I had to do was meet the wrong guy, and suddenly my social life is booming.

Chapter Eleven

Lila and I sit in the administration hall, pretending to do homework in case any teachers walk by. That's the problem with this spot—you always get a seat on one of the couches, but the staff's and headmistress's offices are here so it's not a good place to talk.

I have a book open in my lap and I'm scribbling on some scrap paper. "He took me to Blue Street Diner—"

"So it *was* a date," Lila cuts in.

"Yes." I nod my head. "It definitely was. And he—"

"Did he pay?" She smacks her gum and her voice is strange, combative, like we're arguing a point but we aren't.

"Yes, he paid. But there's *more,* if you'd just listen and not interrupt." I raise my brows at her. She nods. "He asked me out again."

Total silence. Not even chewing. She's just staring at me.

"Lila?" I wave my hand in front of her face. "Hello?"

She slaps at my hand. "Stop it! What did you say?"

"I said yes." I hesitate for a second, then continue. "We're going to a party with Epp and Isabelle Saturday night."

Lila pinches her lips together and her eyes get dark. "Oh, so you have a boyfriend *and* a new best friend now," she replies. "How lovely for you."

I knew she would react like this. "That's right. After nine years of being friends, I'm ditching you and Isabelle's my new best friend. See ya later!" I pat her on the shoulder.

She shrugs my hand off. "That's what it *feels* like. You went out with them last Saturday. You're going out with them this Saturday. You sit with Isabelle in French class."

"Lila, I sat with her *once.* And you and I aren't in the same French class, so it's not like I could sit with you."

"Who's having the party?" she asks in small voice. "Can I come?"

That would be weird, unless I ask Pete to get her a date. But I don't think I can do that yet. And, honestly, I really just want to go with Epp and Isabelle. "I'm not sure . . . I mean, Pete didn't say . . . "

Lila's eyes narrow. She hears exactly what I'm not saying. "You know what? You're a jerk. I spent all day Saturday helping you get ready and I even skipped out of class early to do your makeup yesterday! And all I ask is that you let me come to the party too."

Part of me knows Lila's right, but I still don't want her tagging along. This is my date. And with the way she's been acting recently, so desperate to meet a guy, what if she does something embarrassing? I fiddle with my pencil and we sit in uncomfortable silence for a minute.

"It isn't fair," Lila says. "I'm the one who had the idea about where to go to Driver's Ed, and to go to the St. Ivan's game, so how come you end up with the boyfriend? You didn't even want one, until you met Epp."

"Lila—calm down." She doesn't look at me, and I start to get angry. "Look, *you* convinced me to go after Epp, *you* made me do that stupid article and interview Isabelle. So you can't be mad about what's happened. It's your fault!"

Lila stares at me, hard. "Will you ask Pete if I can come Saturday night?"

"But you don't even *like* Isabelle."

"Neither do you. At least, you didn't until you decided you were in love with her boyfriend and you wanted to use her to hang out with him."

"That's not what I'm doing," I hiss. Two freshmen walk by and glance at us. We're not sitting side by side on the couch anymore; now we're angled toward each other, like we're facing off in a duel.

"You're right," she says. "Now it's worse. You're using *Pete* so you can hang out with Epp."

"I am *not*. I do like Epp, but I know he's a lost cause. So I'm not *using* anyone. I just like hanging out with him and Isabelle. They're fun. And there's nothing wrong with me going out with Pete. He's a nice guy, and I want to get to know him better."

Lila snorts. "Yeah, right."

"Don't be jealous," I say. "As soon as I get to know Pete better, I'll ask him to bring a friend for you and we'll all go out. I promise."

"You promise?" Lila snaps. "Yeah, right. You *promised* me that I'd have access to all the St. Ivan's guys as soon as you did, and now you're ditching me for Isabelle." She avoids my eyes and shoves her books into her bag. "And I'm not *jealous*," she adds. "I just don't like you right now." She gets up and stalks down the hall, her arms swinging angrily at her sides.

- - - -

Lila avoids me for the rest of the day. I don't let it bother me, because I know she'll think things over and realize that dating is complicated, and I can't just invite her along with me everywhere. And she's the one who wanted us to meet guys in the first place, so really this is all her fault.

It's a relief to go to French class last period and see Isabelle. I can tell her about my date, and she'll be pleased about it. But first I need to tell her about the article.

I sit down next to her without waiting to be asked. "Hey."

"Hey." She tucks her hair behind her ears and looks glad to see me. "What's up?"

I tell her the same thing I told Pete. "I talked to the editor of the *Quill* and my article got cut." I hang my head and pretend to be disappointed.

"Really?" Isabelle frowns, genuinely upset. Much more

upset than I pretend to be. "That's too bad. It was going to be so good."

"Yeah. It happens all the time, though," I say. Isabelle nods, but I can see how much she wanted to be in the paper. I'd probably feel the same way. "I do have good news to tell you though . . . "

She gives me a teasing look. "I know. I heard you went out with Pete yesterday."

My cheeks get pink. It's nice to be talked about in a good way. "Yeah. We went to Blue Street Diner."

She smiles and looks genuinely happy for me. Why can't Lila, my best friend, do that?

"Cool," she says. "You guys had fun?"

"Yeah, and he asked me out for Saturday, for the party."

Isabelle gives me a push on the shoulder. "Look at you . . . two dates and you're already a couple! Epp and I are going too."

"Yeah, he told me."

She lowers her voice so no one else hears, and says, "So, you like him, right?" Her tone is a little weird. I can't figure out what it is, but I know yes is the answer she wants to hear.

I doodle on my paper and shrug. "Yeah. I mean, I don't know him that well yet."

"Right, right. I just wanted to make sure." She gives me a funny smile and turns around as Madame comes in to start class.

I tune out the lesson and scribble an apology note to Lila. I consider sticking it in her school mailbox, but then I start to get mad all over again about her not being cool with me having other friends. I wouldn't get mad at her if she hung out with someone else for a change.

So I rip up the note and shove it into the bottom of my backpack. She probably just needs some time to cool off.

⸺ ⸺ ⸺ ⸺

When Mom comes home from work, she's carrying three grocery bags with one arm and dry cleaning with the other. Camille runs up to her and starts jumping on her legs. Mom smiles, not the least bit bothered that the dog is jumping on her while she's carrying eight million things.

I grab the groceries from her and start putting them away, blocking out the sound of her and Camille cooing at each other. There are circles under Mom's eyes, and I wonder if it's all the stuff going on at her job or something else.

"Thanks for helping, chicky." Mom folds the dry cleaning over the back of a kitchen chair and flops into another one. She kicks off her heels and watches as I put everything away. Camille jumps up into her lap and noses for affection. "How was school?"

"Terribly exciting."

"*Taryn.*" She gives me a sharp look.

"Sorry," I say, "but you ask me every single day and it's pretty much always the same."

"I read somewhere that if you ask your teenager lots of personal questions and eat dinner with them every night, they're three times less likely to do drugs."

I close the pantry door with a thud. "Please tell me you're kidding, Mother."

She smiles and laughs, scratching Camille under her chin. "I'm not kidding. But that's not why I ask you questions. I like to live vicariously through you."

"If I were you, I'd shop around for someone more interesting to live through."

"I think you're *very* interesting. Now, what should we have for dinner? I can make that angel hair pasta you like, and I just bought some chicken . . . " Her eyes scan the cabinet doors, perusing them with her X-ray Mom-vision. Her lipstick has worn off and she looks gray and washed out. She used to dye her hair brown, but sometime in the last few months, she gave up and let the gray grow in. I'm still not used to it and try to mentally paint brown over her hair when I look at her.

"I could make a pizza," I offer. "With pineapple and onions. Do we have a pizza crust?"

She nods and points at the fridge. "That sounds perfect. Now, seriously, what's new with you?"

She looks so tired there's no way I can tell her about going to Dad's. It might not be a bad time to tell her about Pete, though. She'll ask a million questions, but I have to tell her before Saturday night. Especially if he's going to pick me up.

I open a can of pizza sauce and begin spreading it on ready-made dough. "Well, I sort of have a boyfriend."

Mom's eyebrows goes sky high. "A *boyfriend*?"

"Yep. A boyfriend." I know I'm exaggerating, but it's so much fun to say, I don't care.

"How can you have a *boyfriend* when you've never even been on a date?" she asks. "Isn't that how it works? You date someone a while, get to know each other, and then you're a couple?"

"That's so old school, Mom." I open a bag of shredded mozzarella and sprinkle it evenly over the sauce. "And, for the record, I've been on two dates. You just didn't know about them."

Her face goes immediately from curious to angry. "Excuse me?"

"Don't get mad," I begin, "but when I went out with Isabelle last weekend it was a double date. Then he took me to Blue Street Diner after school yesterday. Then he asked me out for this Saturday."

"Does this 'he' have a name?" Mom's voice is steady but I can tell she's freaking out.

Luckily I know his last name from his email. "Pete Hargesty."

"Is there anything else you can tell me about him?"

I think a second. "He's got curly hair and he plays soccer."

"I see." Mom strokes Camille's cotton-ball fur and looks thoughtful. "It would have been nice for you to tell me sooner."

I add some chopped pineapple and onion to the pizza and slide it into the oven. "There wasn't really anything to *tell* until yesterday. And I'm telling you now."

"That's true, I suppose."

I set the oven timer for twelve minutes. "And there's a teeny bit more . . . "

"What 'teeny bit'?"

I take a deep breath and cross my fingers. "He's sixteen already, even though he's a sophomore, and he has a car. So he's driving us on Saturday."

Mom stops petting Camille, who gives both of us dirty looks and pokes Mom with a paw to urge her to keep petting. "You know I don't like the idea of you driving around in a car with a boy yet," she says. "It seems so grown-up."

"I *am* grown-up, Mom. I'm fifteen. That's one hundred and five in Camille years."

"I know you are. But your first *boyfriend*! Your first dates." She puts a hand over her mouth. "These are the decisions I hate making alone," she mumbles into her hand.

"You're not making it alone. I'm making it with you."

"Ha-ha."

"C'mon, Mom." We exchange a look and she smiles weakly. "You can meet Pete Saturday when he comes to pick me up, okay?"

"I don't know, chick. How about I drive you? Then at least I know you're not alone in a car with a strange boy."

"He's not *a strange boy*, he's a normal boy who goes to St. Ivan's. And we won't be alone; Isabelle and her boyfriend are going with us."

Mom plays with Camille's collar, fastening it and unfastening it. "All right. Okay. But I get to *meet* him. And talk to him."

"Of course."

Relieved, I set the table and pour milk for both of us. I

pull the pizza out of the oven when the timer dings and test the crust with my fingers. It feels crispy, but not burned. "Dinner's ready."

"What shall we give you, Camille?" Mom asks the dog. "I know you don't like pizza. You like hamburgers."

She gets up and starts rifling through the fridge, looking for leftover hamburger meat. I guess she's not too tired to make dinner for the dog.

The phone rings later while I'm doing my homework. I lunge for it, knocking my notebook off my lap, but I hear Mom pick up downstairs before I can get to it. I pause, trying to hear her talking. It's probably Lila calling to apologize.

"Taryn!" Mom calls up the stairs. "It's for you!" Her voice sounds funny. Tense. It can't be Lila then, it must be my dad.

I have to tell him about Christmas. I pick up the phone and swallow, then say, "Hey, Dad."

"It's Pete."

My whole body contracts for a second as I switch gears. "Oh, hi, what's up?"

"Is your dad on the other line or something?"

"No, I just thought . . . never mind." This is our first phone conversation and it's off to a terrible start.

He coughs. "I have a dance next weekend. Our Christmas dance. Do you wanna go?"

Leave it to Pete to not attempt any preliminary how-are-yous and jump right in. I want to make a joke but he's just asked me to the St. Ivan's Christmas dance. *The* dance! I bet we'll go with Isabelle and Epp. I get to buy a dress!

"Yeah, okay." I keep my tone breezy, so he doesn't think this is the first dance I've ever been invited to.

"Cool," he says. "And, uh, I'll pick you up for the party around eight on Saturday."

I nod, even though he can't see me. "Okay. See you then."

"Yeah. Later."

I hang up and sit on my bed, my hands clasped together in my lap, my entire body tense with excitement. I'm going to the dance! I, Taryn Greenleaf, Eastley sophomore, previously of no-date fame, have a date to the dance everyone wants to go to.

I try to concentrate on my homework but all I can think about is the dance.

Chapter Twelve

I avoid Lila at school the next day.

I justify it by telling myself that if I don't avoid her, she might try and make up with me, and then I'll have to tell her about Pete inviting me to the dance, which will make her mad all over again. And I don't want anything to ruin my cloud of happiness.

In the classes we have together, I arrive late enough that I have to take the last seat in the back row, but not too late that I get in trouble with the teacher. I also make sure I'm packed up and ready to go five minutes before each class ends, so I can dash out of the room before Lila has a chance to talk to me. Instead of meeting her in the student lounge during our free period, I hide out in the library. I do the same thing at lunch, huddling in an empty carrel with my Trig book and sandwich.

It works, but I know I'm being awful. I remind myself she

told me she didn't like me anyway and she might think I'm avoiding her because I'm hurt. And it's not like she's seeking me out, either. She's playing along.

At the end of the day, Isabelle and I walk out of French class together talking about the dance. Ahead I see Lila waiting for me in front of the student mailboxes. Our eyes meet, and she opens her mouth to speak, then closes it when she sees who I'm with.

"You need to go to *Ambrosia* at the mall," Isabelle is telling me. "They have the best dresses. Maybe a dark purple, eggplant color, because that would look really good on you."

"My mom and I are going tomorrow," I say. "I need shoes, too." We walk past Lila, and I feel her watching me, waiting for me to acknowledge her, but I don't look over.

"I have a great pair of black suede heels you can borrow, if you get a dress that goes with them."

"What size? I'm a seven and a half."

"Me too!" She laughs and we walk out the front doors toward the carpool pick-up circle.

I know I'm a jerk for not looking at Lila, for not doing *something*, but it's not like I can casually say hello to her when we're in the middle of a fight. And she hates Isabelle. She wouldn't want to talk to me in front of her.

Isabelle waves good-bye as she gets in a car and says she'll call me later. Only a few weeks ago, in a St. Ivan's bathroom, I overheard her talking about her dress and going to the dance with Epp and I was jealous. And now here I am, going to the dance *with* her, and shopping for my own dress. It's like meeting Epp was some kind of fairy-godmother moment when everything started to change for me.

And as bad as I feel about Lila, I also feel good.

— — — —

Saturday morning Mom and I eat breakfast together. She's acting nonchalant about us going dress shopping, but I know she's excited because she makes blueberry pancakes.

"Isabelle says we need to check out this new store called *Ambrosia*. She said they have great cocktail dresses, and that I'd look good in a dark purple."

"Sounds good." Mom smiles and puts another pancake on my plate. "Do you want to call Lila and ask her to join us?"

I concentrate on pouring my syrup just right. I haven't said anything to Mom about my Lila problem and she's being very nice to invite Lila along on our mother-daughter shopping trip. "Okay. What time are we leaving?"

She looks at her watch. "About eleven. I'm going to take Camille for a nice long walk first so she won't be mad we're leaving her for a few hours. Do you want to join us?"

I stuff some pancake in my mouth so I won't gag. "No thanks."

Mom and Camille leave, and I sit on the sofa in the den staring at the phone. This is my chance to call Lila, apologize, and end our fight. She stormed off on me on Thursday, and I ignored her yesterday. So, in a way, we're even.

I blow out a deep breath and pick up the phone. It rings a few times before I hear a *hello* but it isn't Lila.

"Uh, Mary?" I say. She's home from college already and I still have her bra. "Is Lila there?"

"Yeah—hang on. LILA! PHONE! TARYN!"

Lila picks up. "Yes?" Her voice is cautious and cold.

"Well, you came to the phone. I guess that's a good sign."

She ahems. "What's up?"

My phone hand is sweaty. This is harder than I thought. "You want to go Christmas shopping? My mom's taking me to the mall in a little while."

"I'm going with Mary later," Lila says, in a way that implies how much cooler it is to be going to the mall with one's older sister than one's mother.

"Oh, okay." I pause. "I wanted to tell you something, too."

"What's that?" she asks disinterestedly.

Maybe I'm still mad at her for yelling at me the other day, or for being snippy, because I go ahead and rub it in about the dance. "Pete asked me to the St. Ivan's Christmas dance next weekend. I need to find a dress, and I thought you might want to help."

Lila breathes in and out on the other end. For once, she's not chewing gum. "I'm sure *Isabelle* can give you better advice than I can. Mary needs the phone—I have to go."

She hangs up and I feel my breakfast turn in my stomach.

— — — —

At the mall, I push Lila out of my head and focus on finding my dress. The last time I was alone with my mother at the mall was several years ago, when I actually listened to her advice about clothes. But she has the money, so I need her.

"Let's go in *Clingy Things*," I say, looking sideways at her. Mom thinks this store is trashy, but Lila and I always go in and check out the sparkly tops. "They might have a cute dress."

Mom thinks over her response very carefully. I know she's trying to let me be in charge and not to mother. She presses her lips together, says, "Okay," and follows me in.

I thumb through the racks and see a silver glittery tank dress that would be perfect if I were dancing in a music video, but nothing appropriate for a Christmas dance. They have a great selection of fake diamond jewelry, but Mom manages to talk me out of those by saying I can borrow her pearl studs.

After we wander around to a few other stores, including *Ambrosia,* without finding anything, Mom suggests we go to the special occasion section of Harriman's department store.

"No way." I shake my head. "That's for old ladies."

Mom winces. She loves Harriman's. "Perhaps. But you never know, they might have something we can work with."

Since we've struck out at all my favorite stores, I trudge along after her, feeling myself start to get cranky. Harriman's is a waste of time.

The special occasion section is on the third floor. The carpet is gray and stained, a lot of the dresses are put away wrong on the racks, and the air is stale and smells like paint. My mom is at home here, though, and she immediately zeros in on the younger styles in the back corner. She starts pulling out dresses, regardless of size, and hanging them over the racks face out so we can get a good look at them.

"Look these over and tell me if any of them are even *possibilities*, and we'll use them to narrow our search."

I groan and make faces, but finally point to two that aren't horrible. One is a black strapless taffeta and the other is red velvet with spaghetti straps. Mom studies them, then dives back into the racks, flipping and sorting dresses like she's in a shopping competition.

I lean against a pillar and try not to whine about having to stand around in Harriman's when I could be out scouring all the perfectly good stores in the mall—the ones that are new and shiny and play cool music.

"Taryn," Mom calls from two aisles over. "I've found something."

I weave around racks of ugly, musty dresses to where Mom is standing. Over her arm is a black velvet halter with a pearl collar. I open my mouth to say something but I can't, because I'm too excited by the sight of my first dressy dance dress.

Mom starts walking toward the fitting rooms. "C'mon, slowpoke, let's try it on."

I follow her into a dressing room and don't even ask her to wait outside while I put it on. I pull off my jeans and hoodie and slip into the dress. Mom zips me up and turns me to face the mirror.

Even in my bare feet and ponytail, the dress is perfection. It comes just to my knees, and the back scoops low. It makes me look taller and draws attention away from my not-so-large chest and up to my face.

"This is it," Mom says. "A real jaw-dropper. That's what Grandma used to say—a real jaw-dropper."

"Do you think I could wear black suede heels with it?" I ask. "Isabelle has a pair she said she'd lend me."

"Oh no, you can't wear suede with velvet. I'll buy you shoes. We'll go over to the shoe department right now and find some that match the dress perfectly."

I stand rigidly for a second. Mom hasn't said one word yet about the price of the dress, which I know from peeking at the tag is more that we should spend, and now she's buying me shoes. "Are you sure?"

She puts her arm around me and we admire the dress in the mirror. "Positive."

After buying the exact right pair of heels, we grab some lunch in the food court to celebrate our purchases. Normally I wouldn't allow myself to be seen in the food court with her, but I'm feeling so good about my dress and my date tonight, and she's being so cool, that I don't even care.

We get soup and sandwiches and sit down at a table. I tear into my chicken salad sandwich even though I ate four pancakes this morning.

"I've been looking at your hair, Taryn," Mom says thoughtfully.

I finger my ponytail and it's not even greasy. "What do you mean? I'm going to wash it for tonight."

She laughs. "I mean for the *dance.* Do you want to do

something special? We could make an appointment for you somewhere to have it done."

I've never had my hair done. I should ask Isabelle if girls do that or not, just in case I'm the only one who shows up with fancy hair. "Yeah, maybe. Let me think about it first."

Mom looks pleased I'm considering her idea. It's amazing how different she's been today, how much like her old self. I don't know if it's the shopping trip together, or she's just in a good mood, but even her hair looks less gray.

"You know," I say. "We should really do Christmas this year." Mom's forehead wrinkles at the mention of Christmas, but she listens. "I know we haven't done all the extra stuff for a few years, but it might be fun. It's so quiet just the two of us."

Mom takes a big sip of lemonade. I'm deliberately not saying *any of the extra stuff Dad used to do.* Christmas was much more Dad's thing than Mom's, and after he left Mom scaled everything back. Dad made sugar cookies, and put garlands and lights on the front porch, and strung popcorn and cranberries for the tree. The past two years Mom and I have just had a small tree in the den and a turkey Christmas Day.

"That's a great idea, chick," she says after a minute. She evens sounds like she means it. "My work schedule is a little hectic this week, but if you want a big Christmas, then we'll have one."

I nod and chew on my sandwich. I've been debating something ever since my fight with Lila, and after spending today with my mother, I think I'm making the right choice. "Mom," I say.

"Yes?"

"I'm going to stay here for Christmas. I do need to study, and I'll be at Dad's for Spring Break in March."

She tries to hide how pleased she is, but she fails. The corners of her eyes get wet and she sniffs. "Whatever you want."

"Do you think Dad's feelings will be hurt?"

"He'll be disappointed, I'm sure. But not hurt, no. You wouldn't have hurt *my* feelings if you'd gone. I just would have missed you terribly, that's all."

We finish our sandwiches and discuss some ideas for hairdos that will go with my dress. When Mom asks if I want to hang out awhile longer and get a frozen yogurt, I say yes.

- - - -

At a quarter to eight, dressed in a beaded red camisole and crisp white shirt cinched with a skinny belt, I'm ready for my date. My lips are glossed and my hair is waved. I smell faintly of fruity body splash, which Mom says is sickening but I think is delicious. I've decided not to wear Mary's bra, because it made me too self-conscious last time.

Mom's in the kitchen making dinner for Camille, who's been pouting about Mom and I spending so much time together today.

"Where are you guys going exactly?" Mom asks when I come in. The white shirt I'm wearing is hers, and I see her eye it warily. I didn't ask if I could borrow it. "To the movies again?"

"No, to a party," I say, regretting it instantly.

"Whose party?" Her voice has a hint of panic in it. "Where is it?"

"A friend of Pete's—I'm not sure where. It's no big deal, Mom."

Mom puts her hands on her hips. "*Taryn.*"

"*Mother.*"

Camille lets out a big sneeze and we both look at her. "Mom, it's just a party. I'm going with some friends, and you have nothing to worry about."

Mom hesitates. "Okay, I guess. But I *am* going to worry, Taryn. Every second until you come home. That's what mothers do."

We hear a car pull up and I run to the living room window. "He's here!" I yell.

I watch the car, my heart thudding in my throat. A few minutes go by, and Pete doesn't get out or honk. He just sits there. I wonder if I should I open the front door and wave him in.

"Doesn't he know to come inside?" Mom calls from the kitchen.

"That's just on TV, Mom," I reply. "No one does that anymore."

I hear her snort and say softly, "Everyone knows you have to come in and meet the mommy, don't they, Camille?"

Finally, after several more excruciating minutes, the car door opens and Pete steps out. The car immediately starts rolling backward down our street, and I see him leap back in and stop the car. He gets out again, closes the door, and shakes his head. Then he walks up to our door and knocks lightly with the knocker.

Camille starts barking like FBI agents are crashing through the windows. She runs to the front door and *bark, bark, bark*s at it, trying to sound like she weighs more than ten measly pounds.

"Thanks, Camille. That's very helpful." I try to pick her up, but she dodges me and continues barking. She leaps onto a dining-room chair so she can look out the window as she yaps. "Mother, can you please control her?"

"She's protecting us, Taryn. I don't want to discourage her."

I shake my head and hope Pete finds her charming. I swing open the front door. "Hey, Pete. Come in."

He smiles, a tight, painful smile, and comes inside. I hope his expression is from the constant, high-decibel barking and not from having to come to the door.

"What happened to the car?" I ask.

He turns a nice crayon red. "I, uh, forgot to set the parking brake."

I relax a bit. Pete's nervous too. Maybe even more nervous than I am. "Meet Camille," I tell him. "She's very friendly."

He glances at her and smiles for real. It is hard not to smile at Camille if you don't know her—she's so poofy and fancy looking.

Pete's wearing nice jeans with a button-down shirt and sweater. He looks as though he got dressed for a girl he likes. All the confidence I had about my outfit and hair a few minutes ago disappears and I want to run back up to my room to make sure I look as good as I thought I did.

My mom sticks her hand out to Pete and they shake awkwardly. "It's nice to meet you, Pete. I'm Carol Greenleaf."

"Nice to meet you," he says. "That's some watchdog. What is she?"

Mom beams, practically bursting with pride. "She's a purebred bichon frisé, although we don't keep her trimmed like a show dog."

"She's very pretty." He sounds genuine, but I doubt Pete's the type to enjoy white powder-puff dogs. He seems like more of a mutt lover.

Camille apparently believes him though, because she smiles and hangs her tongue out at him. She's flirting with my date, the little scamp. "Time to go," I say.

"Nice to meet you, Mrs. Greenleaf," Pete says again. I'm proud of him, and I feel a ticklish thrill in my stomach about being picked up for a date by a boy, even though it's not the boy I've been imagining.

Mom opens the door for us. "Have fun, kids. Be home by eleven, Taryn."

I nod. "Okay."

"And be careful." She points her finger at me and I want to die of embarrassment. Luckily Pete is already walking down the porch steps. "I'll be waiting up."

"*Okay*, Mother. Good-bye."

We go down the front walk to his car and Pete opens the door for me. He doesn't just open it and walk around to his side, he waits while I get in and closes the door carefully so my coat doesn't get caught.

The car is cleaner than last time and smells like Lysol. He climbs in and starts it up.

Being out together on an official date feels different, especially with the way Pete is acting. I feel pressure to come up with something to say, something to let him know I'm glad he invited me to the party, but I'm not sure I know him well enough to like him, even though from the way he's acting, it seems he might like me.

After three traffic lights, neither of us has said a word. I guess it's up to me to break the ice. "So, where's the party?" I ask.

He messes with the radio, scrolling through about ten different songs before he finds one he likes. "Behind the mall, in that big development back there."

"Oh." We're both quiet another minute. I rearrange my coat so it's not all bunched up by my seatbelt. "Whose house is it?"

"A guy from school. His name's Vic, but everybody calls him Boomer."

"Boomer?" I'm going to a party at a guy named *Boomer*'s house. Thank God my mom doesn't know that. "How come Epp and Isabelle aren't driving with us?"

"They're at the mall together or something. They'll be there." Pete's head bobs with the music as he talks. It looks dumb, so I look away. "Your dog's kind of a spaz."

"Yeah, she is. We thought she'd grow out of it, but she's almost two. She thinks she's a person—she sleeps under the covers with my mom, with her head on the pillow."

Pete laughs. "What does your dad think about that?"

"He doesn't. He lives in New Jersey."

"Oh." Pete turns down the volume on the radio, like he thinks you can't listen to music and talk about dads in New Jersey at the same time. "You go up there much?"

"Yeah. Some holidays, summer, the usual. We email a lot." I turn the volume on the radio back up. "It's funny—we've always been pretty close, but now we have better conversations over email than we do on the phone."

"That's weird."

I shrug. "It is. But there's less pressure over email. I feel like I can be myself more."

"Email's good that way. I'm not that great on the phone either." He looks sideways at me and we both laugh. He pulls a piece of paper from his pocket and looks at it. "We're looking for Baker Lane."

"Okay." I open my purse and grab a pack of gum. I put a piece in my mouth and hand one to Pete, who takes it.

I point to a sign for Baker, and as Pete turns down the road, we see the party. It's a normal ranch-style development house, but every single light is on and there are lawn chairs set up in the front yard even though it's arctic outside. We have to park way down the street because so many cars are there already.

I realize suddenly I'm about to walk into my first high school party. I have no idea what it'll be like, and I'm glad I'm with Pete, who at least has been to parties before and knows what he's doing.

I follow him to the front door and we walk right in. People

are everywhere, and most of them are holding red plastic cups and hanging on to each other. There's loud rock music coming from somewhere, and a few guys on the couch are singing. In the kitchen I see two girls that are a year ahead of me at Eastley. I smile at them, a friendly smile, but not an I-know-you smile. They're definitely more popular than I am, and I don't want them to think *I* think I'm one of them.

"Want a beer?" Pete semi-yells into my ear.

I shake my head. I've never had a beer and I don't think now is the time to start. I just hope I don't stick out by not drinking, because it looks like a lot of other people are.

Pete opens the fridge, grabs two sodas and hands one to me. The he takes my hand and pulls me into the dining room where it's quieter.

A group of people is playing cards at the table and a girl is dancing by herself in the corner. She's barefoot and has a red cup in her hand. She's singing along with the music and swaying with her eyes closed. Her brown hair has a purple streak down one side.

"That's Boomer's sister," Pete whispers. "She's a senior. Very strange."

I laugh and start to relax. There are so many people here, no one's paying attention to anyone else. I won't stick out.

We roam the party for a while, watching people. Pete says hello to a few guys and introduces me. They all seem to have heard of me before, and two exchange a look with Pete that seems like an approval. I start to wonder if he thinks I'm his girlfriend. The idea makes me uneasy.

"I need to go to the bathroom," I tell him.

He looks at me oddly. "Okay. Do you want me to go with you or something?"

"No! Weirdo." I slap his shoulder, a little harder than I intended. He points toward a hallway and I walk in that direction.

There's a line for the bathroom, so I stand at the end, resting my shoulders against the wall, and think about Pete. He's definitely funny and more talkative tonight. And he seems like a pretty nice guy. But something about him, about him and me, feels off.

There's a flush and the sound of water running, then the bathroom door opens. Carla Wooden walks out.

"Taryn?" She hiccups and puts her hand on my shoulder. She looks different than she does at school, cuter, in her jeans and long sleeve black T-shirt.

"Carla!" I'm surprised to see her here. Especially so tipsy. I figured she hung out at the library on weekends. "Are you okay?"

"I'm *great*." She smiles from ear to ear. "This party rocks. What are you doing here, by the way?"

I know she doesn't mean that the way it sounds, but still, she is a senior and I'm a sophomore. And we're at the same party. "I'm came with Pete," I say proudly.

She looks impressed. "No way! So it worked out? You got the guy? Wow—there's hope for the rest of us."

I panic, realizing she thinks Pete is Epp, the guy I wanted to do the article for. "*No!*" I shriek. "That guy's still dating Isabelle. And they're probably here somewhere."

"Yeah, I saw her out on the deck with some *hunk*." Her eyes get wide. "Oh, *he* must be the one you . . . " She pauses, looking around, and whispers, "*interviewed.*"

Oh my God. Carla thinks something happened between me and Epp! My stomach seizes up and I feel my soda sloshing around in there.

Isabelle's my friend now—I can't have Carla thinking I'd do that to her. What if it got around school? I'd be dead. "Carla, could you forget I ever told you that? Please? Because *nothing happened.*"

"Oh sure, yeah, of course." She smiles at me knowingly and finishes off her drink.

"No, Carla, *really*. Nothing happened."

"I be*lieve* you, okay?" She winks, then shakes her head sadly. "Would've been a great article though. I'm still mad you didn't write it. See you later—I need a refill."

I wait for two more people to get out of the bathroom before it's my turn. I'm shaken up from my talk with Carla so I hurry back out, in case she's out there talking to Pete or something.

I look in the kitchen first but don't see her. I grab another soda from the fridge, and when I turn around, Isabelle's behind me.

"Hey!" I'm glad to see her for two reasons. One, I want to hang out with her, and two, I want to keep her away from Carla.

"Great party, right?" She reaches into the fridge and grabs a drink. "Epp and I just got here—we had to do some

Christmas shopping for his mom and his sister. He can't pick out anything by himself." She rolls her eyes but her voice is proud, like she knows it was a big deal that he asked her advice on what to get his family.

"You didn't miss anything," I tell her, looking around cautiously for Carla.

"Good. Epp's outside saying hi to everyone. You want to grab Pete and come out with us?" She flips her hair back and motions toward the sliding door to the deck.

"Yeah. I'll be right there." I take another long sip of my soda, feeling the caffeine tingle pleasantly in my brain. I need it. I walk into the living room, where I left Pete, but he's not in there anymore, so I keep walking toward the foyer, where I run smack into Epp.

He's leaning against the wall holding a red cup. His dark hair is messy, and he's wearing a bright blue button down, untucked, with jeans. My heart beats faster, even though I tell it not to.

He takes a big swig of his drink. "So, you like my boy Pete, huh?"

I open my mouth to answer, but I can't think of the right thing to say, the thing that will make it sound like I like Pete enough to go out with him, but not enough that Epp'll say something to Pete about it. So I smile and shrug instead.

"He's a good guy," Epp says. "I'm glad he's bringing you to the dance."

"Me too. I got my dress today."

He leans in close to me, and if I didn't know he was crazy

about Isabelle, I'd swear he was flirting. "I'm sure you'll look beautiful."

I look up at his face, trying not to melt like candle wax. His voice, his smell. I feel myself being pulled toward him.

"Hey, Tarrrrryn," Carla calls, wandering into the foyer. "I've been looking everywhere for you. This is your guy, right?"

I pull back quickly, looking from Epp to Carla and back to Epp. "No, this is not Pete," I say slowly and clearly. "This is Epp, Isabelle's boyfriend."

"That's what I meant—Isabelle's boyfriend." She looks him up and down. "Nice to meet you. Taryn thinks you're great, you know. She even, she even . . . " Carla stops herself and starts giggling. "I can't tell you. She made me promise not to."

Epp smiles his huge electric smile. Now he's flirting with *her*. "What? Tell me."

Carla beams up at him. His smile is doing the same thing to her it does to me. She's under his spell.

"She's drunk," I say, putting my arm around Carla and trying to lead her away, toward the bathroom or any place that isn't near Epp. "I'll get her a soda."

"I'm *not* drunk," she protests, shoving me away with one arm. She gazes at Epp. "Taryn likes you. A *lot*. She asked me if she could join the *Quill* just so she could interview you!" She laughs and then shakes her head, looking disappointed. "And then she bailed on me. Didn't even write the article."

Horrified, I look at Epp. He's staring back at me with a

mixture of surprise and embarrassment. "She's confused. She's talking about someone else," I say.

"No, I'm not," Carla says. "You said he was amazing, and you were *right*. No wonder you went after him."

My entire body throbs with humiliation. This is the worst moment of my life. "Go away, Carla, please? Just go away?"

"Fine, I was going to the kitchen *anyway*," she says, somewhat testily. "Buh-bye, Epp. It would've been a great story—the headline could've been something like, 'Quill Helps Sophomore Steal Friend's Boyfriend.'" She laughs and stumbles through the doorway.

Alone in the foyer, Epp and I look at each other. The music and the party are noisy, but it's like the two of us are in some sort of bubble. *He knows I like him.* He knows I faked writing an article to hang out with him. And if he's smart, which I'm sure he is, he's probably figured out why I'm here with Pete.

I open and close my mouth several times like a goldfish. "Epp, I . . . "

He puts up his hand. "Don't say anything. Let's forget this ever happened."

My heart swells in my chest, almost painfully. "Really? You won't tell Isabelle?"

"No way. I don't want her to think you'd do that to her, because you wouldn't right? You guys are friends." The word *friends* is tinged with sarcasm.

"We are friends! Carla's totally wrong. I don't . . . I *don't* like you."

He blushes, actually blushes, like he knows me insisting

that I don't like him is a confirmation of how much I do. "Isabelle's my girlfriend," he says. "And she gets jealous enough as it is. I don't want her knowing about this."

I nod, afraid to speak.

"Besides," he goes on. "You should be writing about—" He stops talking and looks over my shoulder.

I turn around and Pete's standing there, looking at both of us. He hands me a napkin full of pretzels. "Thought you might want these," he says to me. I look up at him, touched. "Isabelle's been looking for you," he says to Epp. "She's out on the porch."

"Okay," Epp says. "I'll head out there." He walks toward the back of the house without even glancing at me.

"You feel okay?" Pete asks. "You look funny."

I feel a lot worse than I look, I'm sure. "I had too much soda," I tell him. "Caffeine makes me jumpy."

"Eat the pretzels. And let's get some fresh air; there are a bunch of people outside I want you to meet."

For a second I consider asking Pete to take me home. I can't hang out with Epp and Isabelle—not if there's a chance Carla might open her big mouth again, or Epp might decide to tell Isabelle. But I don't want to ruin Pete's night, not when he's being so nice. And if I leave before hanging out with Isabelle, she might get suspicious.

So I follow him out to the back deck where everyone's watching some guys playing a game that looks like Ping-Pong with beer in the backyard. It's unbelievably cold and I start shivering. It's all I can do not to stare at Epp, trying to gauge his mood. Will he drink too much and change his mind about telling Isabelle? Or wake up tomorrow and decide she needs to know what a lousy person I am? Or maybe he'll just tell Pete, to warn him about me.

I stick close to Isabelle, mainly to keep Carla from getting anywhere near her, but Isabelle knows a lot of people at the party and she moves in a constant circle, mingling.

She includes me in her conversations and everything, but since I don't know these people, I don't have a lot to say, and I'm so cold and miserable it's hard to keep a smile on my face and pretend I'm having fun.

At one point, when just the two of us are talking, I see Isabelle looking over my shoulder and narrowing her eyes. I turn around and see Epp talking to a girl I don't know.

I look back at Isabelle and say, "Who's that?"

"Some girl from Sinclair," she says, like the girl's no competition for her. "Epp always gets flirty when he's been drinking. It doesn't mean anything—it never does." She looks me dead in the eye for a second, but then immediately starts talking about our plans for the dance next week, and I wonder if I imagined the look.

When my watch says it's almost eleven, I go up to Pete and tell him I need to leave. I'm still shivering and my nose is like an ice cube.

"You look cold," he says, putting his arm around me. He's big and warm, and the sweet gesture makes me feel like a traitor.

"I am. And I told my mom I'd be home in fifteen minutes."

He rubs his hands up and down my arms, trying to make me warmer. "Okay, I'll take you home."

We say good-bye to a bunch of people, including Epp and Isabelle. They're staying and getting a ride home from someone else. When I say good night to Epp, he gives me a completely blank look, almost like we're strangers.

Pete tries to talk on the way home, but I give one-word answers. The nicer he is, the worse I feel. As we pull up in front of my house, I put my hand on the door handle so I can jump out quickly. I don't know if Pete's going to try and kiss me again or not, but I hope not. Earlier I might have wanted him too, but now, it would feel wrong.

He gets out of the car and walks me up to my door, where we stand facing each other like square dancers. "I hope you had fun," he says. "My buddies liked you."

"It was great," I lie. I look down and rifle through my purse to find my key. He puts one hand on my shoulder and lifts my chin up with the other. Before I can react, he leans in and kisses me, holding me in place with his hand. The kiss is soft and perfect, but I can't enjoy it.

"Night," he says, walking down the porch steps and back to his car. "See you Saturday."

Mom and Camille are waiting up for me inside. "Well?" Mom asks, looking at me intently. "How was the party?"

"Fine." I don't look her in the eye. Instead, I reach down and say hello to Camille who sniffs me thoroughly. I toss my coat on a dining-room chair. "I'm really tired, Mom. I'm going up to bed."

She picks up my coat to hang it in the closet. "Tell me about the party first. Did you have fun?"

"It was fine," I say dismissively, starting up the stairs. She and Camille follow me, Camille weaving around my feet.

"Fine? That's it?" She sounds hurt. After all, we did spend the whole day together, and we got along better than we have in ages. But how can I explain to her what a terrible person I am? "What about Pete? Do you like him?"

"Mom, I really can't handle an inquisition right now. Can we talk about it later?"

Mom sniffs. "All right." She goes back down the stairs and I hear her lock the front door.

I feel guilty, but the longer I talk to her, the more likely I am to tell her everything. And I can't possibly tell her what I've done. It's too awful to say out loud to anyone, even my own mother.

"Good night," I call. She doesn't answer.

Chapter Thirteen

I sit at the dining-room table Sunday doing homework but mostly waiting for the phone to ring. I'm positive Pete or Isabelle is going to call to tell me Epp spilled the beans and I'm the world's biggest jerk who doesn't deserve to go to a dance at all, much less with a nice guy like Pete.

I stare at my Latin textbook and relive the scene in the foyer with Carla and Epp over and over again. Even though I want to be mad at Carla, I can't, because I'm the one who was dumb enough to tell her the truth to begin with. And it was the truth—I did do those things.

The worst part of the whole scene was Epp's reaction. He didn't for one single second look happy that I liked him. Or like any part of him, no matter how small, had ever wanted me to. He just looked annoyed that I'd treated his precious Isabelle badly. Which, of course, is exactly how I'd want *my* boyfriend to react if ever put in such a situation, but still. It would have been nice for him to be a little excited that I liked him. I'm obviously not dog food. Pete likes me.

I put my head down on my notebook and sigh. I need Lila to talk this over with, to help me fix things. I can't digest everything by myself. Mom is walking around all huffy and hurt about me blowing her off last night, and even Camille wants nothing to do with me. She hasn't stolen my underwear from the hamper, or chewed on my new shoes for the dance, or done one single thing to antagonize me all day.

I'm alone.

— — — —

I try to make eye contact with Lila several times on Monday, but she ignores me. I notice her hair is different, like she blew it out straight instead of wearing it a little bit curly the way she normally does. I bet Mary did it for her. I bet they spent the whole weekend together hanging out, and that they had a great time at the mall. And I bet Lila didn't stay up most of the night worrying she was going to be outed and humiliated in front of everyone and become the new social pariah of the sophomore class.

In French class, Isabelle motions for me to sit next to her and I do, nervously. But she's her usual cheerful self and doesn't give me any indication that Epp told her anything. She describes the rest of the party, including two guys who got into a fight, and how she and Epp went ice-skating yesterday. I try to listen, but I'm so grateful she doesn't hate me yet that all I can do is nod and smile.

"You want to go to Sam's Diner with me and Epp after school?" she asks. "You can email Pete and see if he can join us. Or I can call Epp."

I doodle on my notebook. Part of me wants to go, because hanging out at the diner with them would be nice. But I can't kick my guilty feelings, and I know I wouldn't have any fun if I went. Hanging out with Pete in front of Epp would be so weird. And so phony. Pete would sense something for sure.

"I can't today," I say. "I've got a *ton* of homework. And this take-home test for Bio . . . "

"No biggy. Epp and I'll probably figure out all the limo stuff for the dance on Saturday. I'll call you and let you know what happens."

"So we're still all going together?" I ask.

She looks puzzled. "Of course. Why wouldn't we?" She opens her notebook and gets out a pen. She leans close and whispers, "Sarah Mickle got asked but I don't want to go with her. She went to elementary school with Epp and she always acts like they're best friends or something."

Sarah Mickle is the blond, bunny-rabbit girl from the football game and one of the most popular juniors at Eastley. I thought she was one of Isabelle's good friends. "Oh, I see."

She plays with her hair. "It's not a big deal or anything, I'd just rather go with you, you know?"

She smiles at me innocently, and I smile back. I'm starting to understand Isabelle a lot better.

After French I try to find Lila. The only way I can get her to talk to me is face-to-face, and I can't wait one more second.

I run to her locker and stand there, panting. When she turns the corner and sees me waiting, her face tenses up. She pulls her books up close to her chest and walks cautiously toward me. She spins the dial on her lock and ignores me.

"Lila, can we talk?"

Silence. She stows some books in her locker and pulls out her coat.

I decide to lay it all out there. It's my only chance. "Lila, I really need to talk to you. Epp knows I like him; he knows I made up the article. He might tell Isabelle. Or Pete. And then I'm screwed."

She turns and looks me square in the face. "I guess you have a problem, then."

"Can we talk? Please?" I grab her arm and she shakes me off.

"It's your mess, Taryn. Clean it up."

"But you encouraged me!" I protest. "You said I should go after him. And now look what's happened!"

She looks at me stonily. "Then you shouldn't ask me for help. I obviously have no idea what I'm talking about." She slams her locker and walks away.

When carpool drops me at home, I see my mom's car in the driveway and feel a sudden sense of relief. I can talk to my mom. Maybe if I tell her everything, every rotten little detail, she'll be able to figure out a way for me to make up with Lila and save my friendships with Isabelle and Pete. I don't even care about Epp anymore. What does he matter if none of my friends will talk to me?

I throw my coat on a hook by the back door. "Hey, Mom!" I call.

"Hello," she calls back, her voice faint and scratchy.

I go in the kitchen and find my mom sitting at the table. She looks terrible—her face is red and blotchy and her eyes are swollen.

"What's the matter? Why are you home early?" I look around for Camille, positive that something must be terribly wrong with either her or the dog. But Camille is on the floor at Mom's feet and looks perfectly fine. "Are you sick?"

"I'm okay," Mom says, rubbing her forehead. "I just had to leave work."

"Why? Did something happen?"

She waves her hand and I see a tissue balled up in her fist. She's been crying. "No, no. I had a fight with your father, that's all."

My whole body goes rigid. What kind of fight would they have had to make her this upset? "Why? What about?"

She shakes her head. "No, Taryn. You don't need to be involved."

"Mom, no matter what, I'm involved. Just tell me. I'm not a kid." I sit down next to her and hand her a fresh tissue.

She wipes her nose and smiles sheepishly. "It's silly of me to get so upset. I haven't let your father get me this riled up in ages. But he always knew how to push my buttons."

"Mom."

"It was just about some money stuff, Taryn." She smoothes her blouse and sits back, letting Camille jump up in her lap. "He missed the payment to Eastley for next semester, and I've called him several times about it. He's paying it, of course, but then we got into some other stuff, like you staying here at Christmas, and it just got heated, that's all."

I stare at her. "You *told* him? Mom! I wanted to tell him myself." I'd meant to call him yesterday, but I was so upset about the party that I'd forgotten.

"I thought you had told him." She looks injured. I know she's being honest and didn't mean to make things worse. "He asked if I minded if you came, and I said of course not but that you'd decided not to. So then he accused me of guilting you into staying here." She looks at me, hoping I'll say I'm staying because I want to.

I soften a little. It's horrible to see my mother unhappy. It's the only thing worse than being unhappy myself. "I'm staying because I want to, Mom. Really."

She smiles and gives Camille a kiss on her head. "Thank you, chicky."

"I'm sorry you had a fight with Dad. Sounds like he was a real jerk." Even though I love my dad, he's the one that left my mom, and I feel like the divorce has been much harder for her than it has for him.

Her face gets stiff and she blows her nose. "Don't talk about your father like that. I wouldn't have told you except that . . . well, here we are."

"We can talk about it if you want to," I say. "You make me tell you every little thing; now I'm going to make you tell *me* every little thing."

Mom cracks a smile. "There's nothing to tell, really. I'm fine. And I'm *happy*, Taryn. I know you worry about me, but I like it just the two of us. I like having time to myself. I like not having to iron your dad's shirts anymore, or listen to him talk about baseball. I know you wish I'd go out more, but I was never very social, and I talk to people all day long at work. When I come home, I want to see you and Camille."

"I just don't want you to be lonely, Mom. I won't be at home forever, you know."

"Yes, you will, because I'm not allowing you to go away to college." I look at her, alarmed, and she laughs. "I'm just teasing, chick. You don't have to worry about your old mom, okay?"

"Okay."

Mom blows her nose one last time and looks at the clock. "We're having leftover beef stew for dinner. You want some now?"

"Yeah, in a few minutes. I need to call Lila."

"Didn't you just see her at school an hour ago?" Mom asks.

"Uh-huh."

"So what do you have to talk about?"

"Homework," I say. "Just homework."

I go up to my room, pick up the phone, and look at it. It doesn't feel very good to be afraid to call my best friend. So instead I reach into my backpack for a piece of paper with a number on it. I take a deep breath and dial Pete's number slowly and carefully, praying Epp didn't say anything to him at school today.

He picks up on the third ring. "Hello?"

"Hey! It's Taryn."

"Oh, hi."

I sigh with relief. He sounds happy I called. "I need to ask you a favor."

"Oh goody," he says. "A favor."

I bite my lip. I don't know why I'm so nervous to ask him. I know he likes me, and he'll probably say yes. "It's about the dance on Saturday. I was wondering if, maybe, you have another friend who wants to go but doesn't have a date?"

"I might. Why?"

"Well, my best friend, her name's Lila, she goes to Eastley with me and I know she'd like to come to the dance, too, and I just thought if you knew someone who didn't have a date yet . . . "

"Uh-huh. Like a setup?" Pete says. He says "setup" like someone would say *stomach flu*.

I have to make this work. This is the only way I can show

Lila I'm serious about making up with her. "Sort of a 'the-more-the-merrier' type thing. Lila's great. You'll like her."

Pete breathes into the phone for a minute, thinking it over. "There's a guy on my soccer team I could ask," he says finally.

"Really? That would be great! She and I haven't been hanging out much lately, and I miss her, and I thought it might be fun for all of us to go together."

"No problem. I'll check with him tomorrow and let you know."

"Okay, thanks."

"Sure. What color is your dress, by the way?" he asks.

"It's black."

"Black," Pete repeats, as if it's very important.

He doesn't say anything else, and I remember him saying he wasn't good on the phone, so I say, "Well, okay, thanks. Good-bye."

"Bye."

I hang up the phone and exhale loudly.

Chapter Fourteen

Tuesday morning I get an email from Pete that reads, *My friend said okay. We'll pick you both up at your house Saturday night.*

He neglects to give me any really important information, like what the guy's name is, how old he is, what he looks like, etc. I consider emailing him back with these questions, but I don't want to sound choosy when he did me a favor, so I just say thank you.

I go looking for Lila during our free period. She's obviously still avoiding me, because she's not in the student lounge, or on the sofas by the front hall, or even in the cafeteria. I finally find her hiding in the library in one of the carrels tucked away against a wall, at the end of a long row of bookshelves. These carrels are hidden from the main part of the library and are the best place to study or hide.

I tiptoe down the row of bookshelves. It's practically an

honor violation to disturb anyone in the carrels, but this is an emergency. When I'm standing behind her, I whisper, "Hey."

She whirls around. "Taryn! You scared the—"

Immediately I hear about fourteen indignant *SShhhhh*s coming from all around us. Lila looks irritated and turns back to her books.

"I need to talk to you, please." I nod my head away from the carrels, motioning to Lila for us to go somewhere else. She looks doubtful. "*Please.*"

Something in my voice must sound desperate, or maybe she's curious, because she makes a huffing noise but gets up and follows me. We go to the far side of the library, where two huge tables are set up in front of a white screen so classes can watch movies. I crouch down on the floor in a corner, my back against a bookshelf. It's a cozy private nook: a good place for a talk.

Lila still looks irritated but sits down beside me. I take a deep breath. "Lila, I am *so* sorry. I know I haven't been very nice lately. I've been a drama-hog, a conversation-hog, an everything-hog. But you are my best friend and I hope you'll forgive me."

Silence. Lila pulls a stick of gum from her pocket and sticks it into her mouth. She chews for a moment, then says, "Ever since you met Epp you've been different. You've been hanging out with snotty Isabelle, and going on dates, and acting like you're too good to hang out with me."

I don't argue; I just nod. She needs me to listen, and that's what I'm going to do.

Lila snaps her gum and keeps talking. "You used to *like* hanging out with me, but now you only call me if you need help getting ready. I don't want to just be your emergency call, Taryn. I want to go out with you too. And—" She stops herself and picks at the carpet with her fingertips.

"Go on," I say.

She looks up at the fluorescent lights and blinks, then looks back at me. "If this is what dating and hanging out with guys is like, then maybe I shouldn't have been so pushy about the whole thing."

"Lila, I'm really sorry," I say again.

She's quiet for a minute. "I know you are."

"And you're totally right about the way I've acted— everything."

"I am?" She looks surprised. I guess she thought I was going to defend my behavior, at least somewhat.

"Well," I say, wanting to be completely honest, "you're *almost* right about everything. Isabelle isn't snotty; she can be pretty cool." Lila rolls her eyes and I feel like I'm losing her again. "Wait, I know you think I'm just saying that, but I'm not. And you'll find out for yourself this weekend."

She stops chewing her gum and gives me a funny look. "What do you mean?"

"Don't get mad, but I got you a date to the Christmas dance. It's a friend of Pete's, and I don't know who he is, or what he looks like, or his name, or anything about him, be- cause Pete didn't give me any details. But we're all going to- gether—you, me, Isabelle, and the guys."

As I'm telling her this, I realize what a potentially terrible idea it is. I've scrounged her up some last-minute date the week of the dance, and I'm forcing her to hang out with Isabelle.

I watch her face as she absorbs the information, prepared to continue apologizing, and possibly start begging. First she looks surprised, then thoughtful. Finally, she smiles.

"I'm going to the St. Ivan's Christmas dance?" she asks. "Really?"

Relief washes over me. I'm going to get my best friend back. "Yep—with some totally random guy. And I'm going with Pete, which is a whole long awkward situation I need to fill you in on. And we get to watch Isabelle and Epp be crazy-disgusting about each other."

Lila's smile suddenly disappears. "You know this doesn't make up for everything, though, right? You really hurt my feelings."

"I know I did. I'm sorry." I gulp and start to get teary.

Lila notices and puts her arm around me. She gives me a hug. "There, all better. I'm sorry, too, by the way. I know I forced you into a lot of stuff that I shouldn't have. And I was acting jealous and jerky."

"Aww," I say, touched. "We were both jerky. But I was more jerky."

"Yes, you were," she says. "But that's okay."

- - ~ ~

I sit behind Isabelle in French class later and tap her on the shoulder.

"Hey," I say. "I hope you don't mind, but Lila's going to come with us to the dance. Pete got her a date."

She raises her eyebrows, but only slightly. I wouldn't have noticed if I hadn't been looking for it. "Sure, great. Who's he bringing?"

"I don't know. He didn't say." I feel foolish admitting I don't even know who he asked. I suddenly remember the night at the movies when Isabelle asked Epp to bring some-one—anyone—as a date for me.

"Oh well, no big deal," she says. "Does she have a dress yet?"

"No, she's going to the mall tonight to find one, I think."

"Tell her we're both wearing black so she doesn't get a black dress. That would be too much." She laughs, but I'm pretty sure she's serious.

"I'll tell her," I say, although I won't.

Chapter Fifteen

The morning of the dance, I wake up to sunshine streaming through the windows and a scary, snarling noise beneath my bed.

I lean over the edge of the mattress, wondering if I should look. With one hand braced on the floor, and one hand on the dust ruffle, I peek under the bed.

Camille is battling with something beige and lumpy. She's ripping it apart; her paws holding it steady as she tears into it. What looks like beige ribbons are wrapped around Camille's ankles.

She's eating my padded bra! Well, Lila's sister's padded bra. "*Camille!* No! Bad!" I yell at her, and shake my finger. But since she's way back under the bed where she knows I can't reach her, she simply looks up, shows me her dangerous teeth, and resumes destroying the bra.

"MOM!" I shout. "HELP!"

Feet thunder up the stairs and my mom rushes into the

room. "Taryn, what is it? Why are you lying like that? Did you hurt your back?"

"No—Camille's eating Mary's bra! She's tearing it apart!"

An enraged snort comes from beneath the bed, following by growling and the sound of ripping. Mom sighs. She gets down on her knees and peers under the dust ruffle with me. Camille is back in the corner whipping the bra around.

"Ca-*millllllle*," Mom says in a baby voice. "Do you want a treat? Mommy will get you a treat if you come out."

Growling. Tearing.

"Ca-*milllllle*. You want a treat?"

Camille pauses and she and Mom stare at each other. The bra straps are so tangled around her paws, she's practically straightjacketed herself.

"Ca-*milllllle*. Do you want some *bacon*?"

These are the magic words. Camille adores bacon. When we first got her, she was so small she couldn't jump up on things. That is, until one day when my mom left a few pieces of bacon on the kitchen table for me. By the time I came down for breakfast, tiny puppy Camille had climbed up onto the kitchen chair, leaped up onto the table, and devoured every last morsel.

Mom snaps her fingers. "I'll get you some bacon if you come out, Camille."

Camille takes a step toward my mom, dragging the bra with her. Step, step, step. She pokes her head out from beneath the bed and sniffs Mom's fingers. Apparently Mom does indeed smell like bacon, because Camille pushes her head into Mom's hands. Mom gathers her up, untangles the remnants of the bra from her legs, and places them on my desk.

"I don't think you'll be wearing that again," she says.

"Mom, we need to *train* her," I say. "She destroys my stuff."

"She just wanted you to play with her, Taryn. If you don't want her to eat your things, don't leave them on your floor. Or keep your door closed."

"I *do* close my door. But she gets in anyway."

Mom gives me a withering look. "I made eggs and bacon. Come down whenever you're ready. Isn't Lila supposed to be here soon?"

"Yes," I snap. "And now I can tell her Camille ate Mary's bra."

Mom walks out of my room, cradling Camille. "Sounds like your sister woke up on the wrong side of the bed this morning, hmm?" I hear her say.

I didn't wake up on the wrong side of the bed, and I couldn't care less about a stupid bra. It's just that my stomach is all butterflies and I can't get them to settle.

Tonight is the dance. The big night. I have a fabulous dress, fancy heels, an escort who likes me, and so far no one other than Epp knows about the terrible thing I did. It's almost too good to be true. I'm afraid to look in the mirror in case another guilt zit has sprung up overnight just to ruin everything. I run my fingertips over my chin and forehead, but my face feels clear.

I throw on my robe and go downstairs to get some bacon

before the dog eats it all. As I'm finishing breakfast, Lila shows up. She looks mildly panicked and is carrying a dress bag over her shoulders, the pink lunch box from my make-over, and a duffel bag.

We head up to my room for a powwow. "You found a dress?" I ask as I help her unload her stuff. "Let me see!"

"No, I did not find a dress, because it's impossible to find a dress in only four days," she tells me bitterly, as if it's my fault her shopping window was so brief.

I squint at her. "Better to need a dress than not need one at all, though, right?"

"I guess so," she admits. "Anyway, I've narrowed it down to two of Mary's dresses. Nothing at the mall screamed *Christmas dance.*"

"Does it have to *scream* Christmas dance?"

"Noooo," Lila says, sticking her lip out. "But this is my first dance. And my first *date.* I wanted something new and beautiful. And instead I'm stuck wearing some old dress of my sister's that doesn't fit me."

"At least you have a real, two-legged sister. And Mary has great taste. I'm sure whatever you brought will be perfect." I point to the bathroom. "Go try them on."

Lila goes to change and comes back wearing a gorgeous strapless dress, with a black velvet sweetheart top, and a black-, red-, and gold-striped taffeta skirt. The hem comes just to her knee and the full skirt is fun and twirly. There's just one problem—the strapless top seems to be sitting at half-mast, and almost the complete top halves of Lila's breasts are spilling out. They look like giant muffins that have baked over the edge of the pan.

"It's nice!" I lie. "Very nice. You just need to pull up the top a little."

Lila wrestles with the neckline, but no matter how she tugs at it, there simply isn't enough fabric to cover her muffins. "I told you," she says.

"I think we're going to have to pass on this one," I reply. "Go try on the other one."

She comes back out in a dark red knee-length dress with a V-neck. Her breasts are covered this time, but they look like they're suffocating. Like they're fighting for air and might burst out of her dress at any moment and make a run for it.

"This one's better, right?" she asks hopefully.

"Wow," I say, trying to be tactful. "It's a great color. Could you wear a different bra with it?"

Lila glares at me. "In case you haven't noticed, my boobs are twice as big as Mary's. I could wrap myself in duct tape and still be busting out. Literally. It's this or my uniform."

I throw my hands up in the air. "All right, then this is the dress. It really does look pretty on you."

"Yeah, pretty horrible," Lila mutters. "I hope Pete's friend is nice. Do you think he'll be nice?"

"No, he'll be a complete and total jerk. And he'll have warts. I'm pretty sure Pete said something about the guy having warts."

"Oh God, he probably will. And bad breath. And he'll step on my feet and be so short his face will be boob-height."

"Stop it—let's think positively. Isn't that your motto?"

She nods. "You're right, here goes." She closes her eyes and inhales, then exhales slowly. It sounds sputtery, like a car that won't start.

"You okay?"

She opens her eyes and looks at me. "Though I cannot breathe, this will still be the greatest night of my life."

"That's better! And it will be *our* greatest night—you and me together." I put my arm around her shoulders and we stand in front of my full-length mirror, admiring ourselves: me in my pajamas and robe and Lila in her too-small dress.

"It's going to be awesome," she says, sucking in her breath again. "Awesome."

⸻

By seven o'clock, Lila and I are pacing around the living room waiting for the limo to arrive. Mom took us to a salon earlier to get our hair done, and the stylist twisted Lila's hair into a low, curly bun and set mine in wide waves, with a few bobby pins holding back the front pieces so they're out of my face.

I honestly don't think I've ever looked better. And Lila looks very pretty and Christmasy, if a tad busty, in her red dress. My mom is snapping pictures like it's my wedding day.

"Mom, that's enough. And only one or maybe *two* pictures when the guys get here."

ISABELLE'S BOYFRIEND   165

"You'll thank me when you're older, chick." She gives me a pointed look. "You know how much you love that picture of you standing by the mailbox in your uniform on your very first day at Eastley? Well, you didn't want me to take that one, either."

I shake my head but don't argue with her. I'm jittery about tonight, about everyone getting along with each other, and part of me is still worried that Epp has outed me and Pete won't show up, or that he *will* show up and throw tomatoes at my house.

I see Camille hovering suspiciously around the good sofa in the living room, rubbing one lifted leg against its skirt. *"Camille!"* I yell. *"Don't pee on anything!"*

"Taryn," my mom chastises. "She's scratching her leg."

"Oh. Well, keep an eye on her."

Mom and Lila look at me like I've lost my mind, but before I can remind them what she did at Isabelle's house, the limo pulls up and all of a sudden it's happening. Lila and I run to the window and peer out. In the darkness, we see two guys get out of the limo. We run back to sit on the sofa and act like we've been casually chatting in our formalwear. Camille begins her guard-dog barking, and Mom shushes her and opens the door.

Two well-dressed guys walk in. Pete, in a navy blazer, crisp white shirt, and bright blue tie, looks great. His hair is more styled than usual—flatter and less puffy. I'm not sure if it's the dressy clothes, my excitement about the dance, or my relief that he showed up, but I'm really happy to see him.

His friend, luckily, is none of the horrible things Lila imagined. Instead, he's about Pete's height, a little on the skinny side, and very average-looking, with fair skin, dark hair, and no visible warts. He's wearing a blazer and khakis like Pete, but with a Christmas tie that has Santa stuck trying to get down a chimney.

Lila catches my eye and I see she's relieved. I'm relieved too, because now I know I can enjoy the evening. We both have presentable dates that have shown up, and neither of them knows about the article.

"Where are Epp and Isabelle?" I ask Pete. As nervous as I am to see Epp, the evening won't feel completely real until I see them dressed up together, the way I imagined it back in the St. Ivan's bathroom.

"We're picking them up next," he says. "They're at Isabelle's."

Pete and my mom say hello, and I can tell she thinks he looks nice in his blazer. Camille evidently remembers him because she doesn't growl at him; she just sniffs the cuffs of his pants.

"This is Derek," Pete says, introducing him to my mom, Lila, and me all at once.

"And this is Lila," I say, just as awkwardly, since Pete hasn't met Lila either, and I'm not sure Derek knows which of us is which. No one shakes hands or anything, and we all nod at each other like we're not sure what to do next.

"Those are lovely corsages," my mom says, looking at the plastic flower boxes both guys are holding. "Why don't you pin them on the girls and I'll take a few pictures?"

I shoot my mom a warning look but she pretends not to notice and fiddles with her lens cover. There's no stopping her when she has the camera in her hands.

Derek fumbles opening his box and stands there with it, waiting for Lila to walk over to him, I guess. She looks confused but finally figures it out and goes and stands in front of him. He pins the corsage on her dress, focusing intently on her chest as he's pinning. When he's done, he looks up at her eyes, and she smiles at him. His cheeks flush but he smiles back.

Pete walks over to me and opens his box. He bought a wrist corsage, which, although safer, is less exciting to put on. "Nice dress," he says quietly, leaning in toward me so no one else will hear. "You look really pretty."

My ears get red. I know if Pete says something like that, it's because he means it.

My mom takes an unacceptable number of pictures until finally Lila and I push the guys out the door and walk to the limo. There's no graceful way to climb into a limousine in a tight formal, but I try. We all sit stiffly in our fancy clothes—Pete and I in the backseat, and Lila and Derek along the side seat.

They immediately start talking about soccer, which he plays. Lila asks a million questions and tells him she's a huge soccer fan, which is a big fat lie. But he eats it up and they sit inches apart, despite the extra four feet of room on the seat.

We pick up Epp and Isabelle, who climb into the limo

looking like royalty: Epp in a dark suit and a deep red tie and Isabelle in her low-cut black silk dress. Her hair is arranged in long loose curls and there's a sparkly barrette holding it back on the right side. She looks like a movie star, with Epp as her leading man.

This is the first time Lila has seen Epp up close, and she gives me a look that says, "Ah-ha. *Now* I get it."

Epp and Isabelle take over the backseat, so Pete and I skooch up along the side seat with Lila and Derek.

"You both look gorgeous!" Isabelle says to Lila and me. "I'm so excited for the dance, aren't you?"

I tell Isabelle she looks amazing, and Lila grunts her agreement. I elbow her to remind her to play nice. We have a long evening ahead of us, so we might as well get along.

"I'm Epp," Epp says, introducing himself to Lila. He nods hello at Derek, and Derek looks slightly embarrassed he forgot to introduce his date. "Hey Derek, Pete."

Then, without even acknowledging me, Epp immediately asks Pete about a Spanish test they had yesterday. I feel myself blushing, wondering if anyone else noticed that Epp completely ignored me. No one seems to. Isabelle asks me where I got my shoes, and Lila and Derek go back to their conversation about soccer, so I just concentrate on being cheery and answering Isabelle's questions.

When we arrive at the dance, I put the car ride out of my mind. Walking into the hotel is like walking into a dream. We enter a huge old ballroom with a fancy gold ceiling.

There are white Christmas lights everywhere and stacks of fake presents on either side of the ballroom doors. Small tables with white cloths and votive candles line the edge of the dance floor. There's a deejay playing "Rockin' Around the Christmas Tree" and the dance floor is already packed. It's exactly what I'd pictured in my head.

We check our coats and linger for a minute by the stacks of presents.

"It's beautiful," Lila says, admiring the ballroom. Derek nods his agreement, but he's mostly looking at Lila and not the ballroom.

"Look," Epp says to Isabelle, "there's Joey. I need to talk to him for a sec." He grabs her hand and pulls her with him. She glances back at us apologetically as she's dragged along. I would think it was really rude if I hadn't already figured out he was planning to stay away from me. For some reason, being avoided so deliberately is more embarrassing than him knowing I made up the article.

"Want something to drink?" Pete asks me. "It's hot in here."

The four of us wander over to the refreshment table and grab drinks. They have non-alcoholic eggnog, cranberry juice mixed with club soda, sparkling water, and regular sodas. They also have a huge assortment of Christmas cookies and cheese and crackers in case we get hungry dancing. I grab a glass of cranberry and soda and watch everyone coming in the doors. Most of the girls are more dressed up than their dates, with their hair and nails done, high heels, and beautiful shiny dresses. The guys are mostly in blazers.

Epp is one of the few in a dark suit. I glance at him on the dance floor, where he and Isabelle are fast dancing. They look comfortable, like they've danced together before.

Lila and Derek start discussing their favorite movies. In the hour they've known each other, they've covered everything from school to sports to vacations. By the end of the night, they'll have exhausted every available topic. Lila's doing most of the talking, but Derek doesn't seem to mind.

Pete and I talk about the dance a little, and he introduces me to a few of his friends who walk by, but we don't have as much to say as Lila and Derek do.

We take our drinks and sit down at one of the tables by the dance floor. Derek and Pete start discussing their soccer team's winter practices, which is a boring discussion about running hills in the mud, so Lila and I check out everyone dancing. We pick out our favorite hairstyle (a blond girl's French twist with a large orchid in it), our favorite dress (long and red, with a floaty chiffon skirt), and our favorite guy (Epp).

"He really is perfect," Lila whispers to me.

"Who? Derek?"

She laughs and chokes on her cranberry juice. "*No,* although I really like him. I meant *Epp.* He does have something weirdly magnetic going on."

"Yeah, I know." I watch him on the floor with Isabelle. "But he hates me now. Did you notice he didn't say a word to me in the limo? He probably won't come near us all night."

Lila shrugs. "So? The four of us will have fun."

"I know, but I want to hang out with him and Isabelle too." I say this, but I don't know why I want to hang out with them. Being near Epp and having him despise me makes me sick to my stomach. "What do you think of Isabelle?"

Lila makes a face. "She's all right. But I don't think she's as nice as you think she is."

"Why? Maybe we're just jealous of her. It's hard not to be."

"Yeah, maybe." Lila laughs. "But I think her being friendly with you was just convenient. You were putting her in the school paper, and she probably figured out you liked her boyfriend and wanted to guilt you out of it by being nice."

I think that over. "But she was still nice to me after I told her the article got killed."

"Because you'd started dating Epp's friend. And maybe she liked hanging out with you because her other friends like her boyfriend, too."

"Epp did say she gets really jealous," I tell her. "But he's a huge flirt, so no wonder."

Pete leans over the table and interrupts us. "Wanna dance?" he asks me. The deejay has finally put on a slow song and couples on the dance floor are glued together.

With a nervous glance at Lila, I get up and follow him to an open spot on the floor. He puts his arms around my waist and pulls me close. Too close. My forehead is pressed into his shirt collar, so I turn my face sideways. He smells like eggnog. We sway back and forth to the music.

"Are you having fun?" he asks.

I start to nod then realize I'm smearing makeup on his jacket. "Yeah, it's great. Thanks for inviting me."

"You seem quiet. You know, for you."

"I'm just watching everybody," I say. "There's a lot to look at."

"Oh."

We dance silently for a minute. Even though Pete is the right height for me in heels, and he isn't doing any fancy moves, our bodies don't seem to be moving side to side the same way. Our dancing doesn't feel smooth.

"I want to ask you something," Pete says, his mouth by my ear. His voice is serious and my heart starts pounding. "Will you go out with me?"

This time I know exactly what he's asking. I keep my cheek pressed against his coat and don't look up at him. I have no idea what to say. This is the moment I thought I wanted—a great guy, a St. Ivan's guy no less, asking me to be his girlfriend.

We keep swaying to the music and I don't push him away or reply. I stay right where I am, dancing. Thinking. Trying to figure out what to do.

After a long minute he says, "It's okay if you don't want to." But I can hear in his voice that it's not.

"No, I . . . " I pull away and look up at him. He's not looking me in the eye, but he's trying. His face and ears are red and I feel a stab in my heart that I'm hurting him. "Pete, I . . . ," I start to say again.

Something I see out of the corner of my eye stops me. On my right, a guy in a dark suit and a girl in a black dress are making out. It's Isabelle and Epp, and they look like they might need the jaws of life to tear them apart. How can I tell Pete that even though having him to hang out with is fun, and I do like him, I don't feel *that* way about him?

I look on the other side of us where Derek and Lila are dancing. Derek's got his hands on her shoulders and they're doing an awkward box step where they trip over each other every two seconds. For a guy who plays sports, Derek isn't very coordinated. But they're smiling and cracking up, and I can tell they like each other. They don't even care how stupid they look.

I glance up at Pete, whose arms are wrapped around me. Somehow we're still dancing.

"I like you," I say, "but I don't think I want to go out, go out." It sounds stupid but it's all I can say. I don't want to lead him on. And the truth is, if he tried to kiss me again, I wouldn't want to, because I know I don't like him that way. So it wouldn't be fair for me to keep going out with him.

Pete frowns and I feel his body stiffen. "I don't get it," he says. "I thought that's what you wanted."

I look down. I guess I have been leading him on: accepting dates, letting him kiss me, going to the dance with him. But I never acted like I really *liked* him. Did I?

He loosens his arms so we can face each other. A fast song has come on and we look stupid slow dancing, but neither of us moves.

"I mean, Epp told me what happened at the party last weekend," he says.

My throat closes up and I feel like I'm about to choke. Epp *told* him? Why did he tell Pete and not Isabelle? And why is Pete still speaking to me if he knows? "H-he did?"

"Yeah. He said you guys talked, and you said you really liked me and that you wanted me to ask you out." He lowers his voice as he's speaking, embarrassed just saying the words.

I can't believe it. Why would Epp do that? "I, uh, well, I think he misunderstood. What I said was that I *like* you, but I don't really want to go out with anyone right now."

Pete stops pretending to dance and drops his arms. We stand there, in the middle of fifty gyrating couples on the dance floor, looking as out of place as people wearing sneakers on a skating rink. "Then why did you come to the dance with me?" he asks.

He sounds wounded. I never stopped to think that Pete might see me coming to the dance with him as something special. But obviously he did.

"Pete, I'm *so* sorry. I thought it would be fun, you know . . . " I look at him, hoping he'll understand I didn't realize I was being selfish. But of course I realized it; Lila even told me. And I did it anyway.

"I get it," he says. "You just wanted to come to the dance—you didn't care with who. And you wanted to bring your friend so you two could hang out together and have fun. Well, I hope you do." He turns abruptly and walks off the dance floor, leaving me standing there alone.

I let out the breath I've been holding and stumble over to our table. I feel awful. I've just ruined his dance. And the worst part is, I know how it feels to like someone so much and not have them like you back.

I wait for Lila to come off the dance floor, where she and Derek are doing some kind of fast dance that resembles two gorillas waving their arms at each other. When they return, they're both shiny and giggly and Derek is holding her hand.

I know I'm being selfish yet again, but I need my best friend. "Derek, I'm going to steal Lila for a sec, okay?"

He nods. "Sure. Want me to get you guys some drinks? Where's Pete?"

"Uh, he's over at the drinks table already." I make a frantic gesture at Lila and she follows me out of the ballroom and down the hallway. Our heels are ridiculously loud on the marble floors.

Lila looks at me worriedly. "Taryn, what? What is it?"

"Shhh, not here." There's no point trying to talk in the hallway; it'll echo throughout the entire building.

Finally I see a sign for the ladies' room and pull her in with me. It's one of those fancy lounge types with a sitting room, and after checking under the stalls for feet, we plop down on a long upholstered bench.

"Are you all right?" she asks me.

"Yeah, I'm fine." I remember my vow not to be a conversation hog and make myself ask about her. "Are you? Are you having fun?"

"Yes!" Lila says. "Derek's awesome. He's funny and he *gets* me."

I bite my tongue to keep from asking how a guy she's

only known a few hours could possibly *get* her. She's got a dreamy look on her face and I realize I now have to be envious of Isabelle *and* Lila. They've both found their guys.

"That's great," I say, feigning enthusiasm. I owe Lila that, at least. "He really seems to be into you."

She smiles and sighs deeply, not even noticing her too-tight dress anymore.

I can't take it any longer. I have to tell her this second or I'll explode. "Pete asked me to go out with him," I blurt out, putting my head in my hands.

"Wait—why is that bad?" Lila scoots over and puts her arm around me. "He's cute, and he seems really nice."

"I know, but I don't liiiike him."

"I thought you said you did?" Lila asks, confused. "A little bit, at least."

"Yeah." I stare at my gorgeous shoes, wishing I could click my heels together three times and be home. "But I don't *like* like him. And apparently Epp told him I did, so he was all pumped to ask me out, and then I said no. So he told me to have a good time and just walked off! I feel terrible."

"It's not your fault you don't like him back," Lila says. "And you shouldn't be with someone you don't really like. Sometimes, things aren't meant to be."

This is the new, lucky-in-love Lila talking. I want to remind her of how just a few weeks ago she was throwing us at any guy in Driver's Ed, and now she believes in soul mates. But just because I'm insanely jealous her first date has turned into a serious boyfriend already, I don't need to take my frustration out on her.

"You're right, Lila," I say. "You are so right."

"It'll be okay," she says, giving me another shoulder squeeze. "He'll get over it."

"Not in the next two hours."

"C'mon." She pokes me. "I'm not going to let you wallow. We're at an awesome dance. Let's enjoy it!"

I shake my head. "I don't deserve to enjoy it—I'm a horrible person. You go hang out with Derek, and I'll come out in a little bit, okay?"

"Really? You want me to leave you in here?" she asks. She sounds doubtful, but I know she wants to be with her date. Why should I ruin her evening too?

"Really, *go.*"

Lila smiles gratefully and leaves. I sit on the bench, feeling like a total idiot. I thought that going to a dance and having a boyfriend were the most incredible, stupendous things in life, and it turns out I'd probably be happier sitting in the biology lab right now, wearing my comfy uniform and learning about mitosis. And I'd definitely be less of a jerk.

After a few more minutes of serious moping, I get up and sort through the complimentary toiletry basket on the counter. I powder my nose, apply lip balm, and eat about forty breath mints. None of it makes me feel better.

I hear some girls in heels clackity-clacking down the hall, so I duck into a stall and close the door. I don't feel like seeing anyone.

"I can't believe it," a girl says, coming into the bathroom. "I can't *believe* it!"

"I know! Isn't it amazing?" says another. It's Isabelle. It's Isabelle, and I'm stuck in the bathroom stall again.

"What did you say to him?" the friend asks.

"What do you think? I said, 'I love you too.'" The joy in Isabelle's voice is tangible. It's like the warm sun on your back at the beach. Except it's not on my back, it's on Isabelle's.

Isabelle and Epp are in love. He never would have liked me as a girlfriend, and now that he knows what a jerk I am, he doesn't even like me as a person.

I didn't think it was possible, but I've actually sunk to a new low.

Isabelle and her friend fix their hair in the mirror and gossip for a few minutes. This time I don't come out. I stay in my stall until they leave.

When I finally go out in the hallway, semicomposed and determined to live through the rest of the evening, I see Epp coming out of the men's room. We lock eyes, and I can tell he's talked to Pete. He's looking at me like I ran over his dog.

"Hi." I fidget in my dress, feeling too pretty, too dressed up, to have an ugly conversation.

"Hey." He glances down the hall, probably looking for Isabelle.

"She just left," I tell him. "She's back in the ballroom."

He nods and starts to walk away. I know I should keep quiet, but I open my mouth before I can stop myself.

"Why'd you tell Pete I like him? He asked me out and I

said no, and now I feel terrible." My voice comes out harsher than I mean it to.

Epp looks taken aback. "What'd you want me to tell him? He walked into the foyer at the party when you and I were talking. He thought I was hitting on you." He gives me a disgusted look, one that says, *Not that I would.*

"Oh," I say quietly. I want to run back into the bathroom stall. He was trying to cover for me, and here I am yelling at him.

"Pete's a really good guy," Epp says. "You should give him a chance."

I look down at the floor. I'm being lectured to like a guy by the guy I really like. "I know he is."

There's a question burning my insides, one that I have to ask, and even though I know I *shouldn't* ask it, this might be my only chance. "Do you think, if you hadn't been dating Isabelle when we met, you might have liked me?" I feel my face get red. I don't know why I'm doing this to myself.

Epp looks blank for a minute, then shrugs and says, "I don't know."

That's it. That's all he says—*I don't know.* I clear my throat. "Well, Isabelle's probably looking for you, so you'd better get back."

"Yeah." He pauses and plays with the sleeve of his suit jacket, like he's about to say something important. "We're getting a ride home with my friend Joey. Don't wait for us."

The next two hours are painful.

Pete spends a lot of time talking to his buddies, leaving me to hang out with Lila and Derek. He does come back and check in every now and then, and I can tell he's not trying to be mean, he just doesn't know what to say to me.

Epp and Isabelle are always on the dance floor or at other tables talking. I know Epp won't come anywhere near me ever again, since he must be positive now that I'm a crazy person who's obsessed with him.

Luckily, Derek and Lila are having such a good time they don't seem to notice I'm their third wheel. The later it gets, the cozier they get, with their chairs smooshed together and Derek's arm permanently wrapped around Lila's shoulders.

I act like I'm having fun too, because I know Lila's having a great night. But when Pete comes by and asks us if we want to go home, I say yes even though I know it's early and I should try and stick it out.

I get dropped off first. When the limo pulls up in front of my house, Pete opens the door and gets out of the car with me. I was positive he wouldn't, so I panic and trip as I'm stepping out. He catches my arm but lets go immediately. I wave good-bye to Lila and her lover boy, who look like they're about to start making out.

I turn toward my house and do a double take. While I was at the dance, my mom decorated for Christmas. She put candles in every window, a wreath on the front door, and a fully decked-out tree in the dining room. My chest gets tight, because I know she did it for me.

I don't want Pete to walk me up to the porch where he kissed me last week, so halfway up the sidewalk I turn and face him. "I'm really sorry I ruined your dance. I didn't mean to, honestly."

He shoves his hands in his pockets and looks at his feet. "You didn't ruin it."

"I want to be friends, because I really do like you." I hope he can tell I'm sincere, and not just trying to make him feel better. "And, anyway, it looks like Lila and Derek might be hanging out together a lot."

He nods, but stiffly. "Sure."

I wish I liked him. I wish things had turned out differently. But they didn't. "Well, good night. And thanks for taking me."

He smiles and shrugs. "It was memorable, at least." He turns to get back in the limo, and I wave at its tinted windows, even though I'm sure Lila's too busy to notice.

I open the front door and Mom appears, carrying Camille. "You're home early," she says, a question in her voice.

I ignore the question and let Camille smell me. "The house looks beautiful, Mom."

"Thank you," she says, locking the door behind me. "Why are you home early?" she asks again.

I kick off my shoes and toss my purse on the dining-room table. "Because I'm a selfish, awful human being and I don't deserve to have fun at a dance." Now that I'm safe at home, I feel the beginning pricks of tears behind my eyes.

Mom raises her brow. "Excuse me?"

A few drops escape and I turn away from her, but not before she sees them.

"Oh, Taryn," she says. "What happened?"

I suck in a breath to stop the tears. "It's a long story. Let me put on my pajamas first." I reach up to start unpinning my hair. "Will you make me some hot chocolate?"

Mom looks worried but nods, pleased I want to talk. She and Camille go into the kitchen. "Take your time," she calls.

I pass the Christmas tree at the bottom of the stairs and pause. The room is dark except for the Christmas lights, and the pine smell is strong. The tree must have been freshly cut. Our ornaments, many of them handmade by me when I was younger, glimmer on the tree.

The tears start flowing again as I climb the stairs and unzip my dress. I leave the lights off in my room, except for the tiny candles Mom put in the windows.

I'm crying hard, but it's just tears and no hiccups. I'm crying because I feel sorry for myself, and because I'm embarrassed, and because I liked a guy who didn't like me. The whole thing is so stupid, really; everything I did because of Epp.

I throw on a pair of Eastley sweatpants and a T-shirt. Then I go into the bathroom to blow my nose and wash my face so I'll stop crying. When I've finally stopped, and my eyes are puffy but dry, I loop my hair into a bun and pad downstairs in my slippers.

Mom and Camille are curled up on the sofa in the den. My hot chocolate is waiting for me on the table.

"You did a great job with the decorations, Mom," I say cheerfully. "The tree looks like the best we've ever had."

I can see from her face she knows I've been crying, but she doesn't say anything. She just scratches Camille's head, and says, "Thank you. We worked pretty hard this evening."

"I would have helped, you know. You didn't have to do it all by yourself."

"That's okay. I wanted to do it for you, as a surprise. I know having a big Christmas means a lot to you." She hesitates, then continues. "You can still go to New Jersey, if you want. You can even decide to go at the last minute and it'd be fine with your dad and me."

I shake my head, no. I made the right decision last weekend. "I want to stay here, at home."

"Okay." She smiles tentatively. "Do you want to tell me about the dance?"

I pick up my cocoa and take a cautious sip. It's hot, but not too hot. I stretch my feet out on the ottoman next to my mom's and lay back. Camille snuggles down between us with her head on Mom's lap and her butt squished against me.

"I'm not sure you want to know," I say honestly. I want to tell her the whole story, but I'm ashamed of what she might think of me. I'm ashamed of myself, really.

Mom bites her lip. "So, it went pretty badly?"

"Yes."

"Are you and Pete still seeing each other?"

"*No*. But Lila and her date are practically engaged. They

didn't stop talking the entire time. I spent half the night watching them gaze at each other, and the rest hanging out in the bathroom with my shoes off."

Mom laughs. "So things didn't turn out the way you wanted, huh?"

"Not exactly." I think about Epp and all the scheming I did to get him. It didn't work out, clearly, but if it had, would I have wanted to go to the dance with him tonight knowing I'd taken him from Isabelle? She might not be the friend I thought she was, but she loves him, and she doesn't deserve that. "I don't think I knew what I wanted. It's a looooong story." My voice catches like I might start crying again.

Mom reaches behind her and pulls the afghan from the arm of the sofa. She spreads it out over our legs, and fluffs the pillow behind her back. "I'm not going anywhere, chick."

I take a deep breath and snuggle down under the afghan. "Well, it all started a few weeks ago when I met Isabelle's boyfriend . . . "